The Wasp Factory

The Wasp Factory

Iain Banks

MACMILLAN LONDON

for Ann

ISBN 0 333 36380 9

First published 1984 by
Macmillan London Limited
London and Basingstoke

Associated companies in Auckland, Dallas,
Delhi, Dublin, Hong Kong, Johannesburg,
Lagos, Manzini, Melbourne, Nairobi,
New York, Singapore, Tokyo, Washington
and Zaria

Printed in Great Britain by St Edmundsbury Press
Bury St Edmunds, Suffolk

Reprinted 1984

Contents

1: The Sacrifice Poles

I HAD BEEN making the rounds of the Sacrifice Poles the day we heard my brother had escaped. I already knew something was going to happen; the Factory told me.

At the north end of the island, near the tumbled remains of the slip where the handle of the rusty winch still creaks in an easterly wind, I had two Poles on the far face of the last dune. One of the Poles held a rat head with two dragonflies, the other a seagull and two mice. I was just sticking one of the mouse heads back on when the birds went up into the evening air, kaw-calling and screaming, wheeling over the path through the dunes where it went near their nests. I made sure the head was secure, then clambered to the top of the dune to watch with my binoculars.

Diggs, the policeman from the town, was coming down the path on his bike, pedalling hard, his head down as the wheels sank part way into the sandy surface. He got off the bike at the bridge and left it propped against the suspension cables, then walked to the middle of the swaying bridge, where the gate is. I could see him press the button on the phone. He stood for a while, looking round about at the quiet dunes and the settling birds. He didn't see me, because I was too well hidden. Then my father must have answered the buzzer in the house, because Diggs stooped slightly and talked into the grille beside the button, and then pushed the gate open and walked over the bridge, on to the island and down the path towards the house. When he disappeared behind the dunes I sat for a while, scratching my crotch as the wind played with my hair and the birds returned to their nests.

I took my catapult from my belt, selected a half-inch steelie, sighted carefully, then sent the big ball-bearing arcing out over the river, the telephone poles and the little suspension bridge to the mainland. The shot hit the 'Keep Out – Private Property' sign with a thud I could just hear, and I smiled. It was a good omen. The Factory hadn't been specific (it rarely is), but I had the feeling that whatever it was warning me about was important, and I also suspected it would be bad, but I had been wise enough to take the hint and check my Poles, and now I knew my aim was still good; things were still with me.

I decided not to go straight back to the house. Father didn't like me to be there when Diggs came and, anyway, I still had a couple of Poles to check before the sun went down. I jumped and slid down the slope of the dune into its shadow, then turned at the bottom to look back up at those small heads and bodies as they watched over the northern approaches to the island. They looked fine, those husks on their gnarled branches. Black ribbons tied to the wooden limbs blew softly in the breeze, waving at me. I decided nothing would be too bad, and that tomorrow I would ask the Factory for more information. If I was lucky, my father might tell me something and, if I was luckier still, it might even be the truth.

I left the sack of heads and bodies in the Bunker just as the light was going completely and the stars were starting to come out. The birds had told me Diggs had left a few minutes earlier, so I ran back the quick way to the house, where the lights all burned as usual. My father met me in the kitchen.

'Diggs was just here. I suppose you know.'

He put the stub of the fat cigar he had been smoking under the cold tap, turned the water on for a second while the brown stump sizzled and died, then threw the sodden remnant in the bin. I put my things down on the big table and sat down, shrugging. My father turned up the ring on the cooker under the soup-pan, looking beneath the lid into the warming mixture and then turning back to look at me.

There was a layer of grey-blue smoke in the room at about shoulder level, and a big wave in it, probably produced by me as I came in through the double doors of the back porch. The wave rose slowly between us while my father stared at me. I fidgeted, then looked down, toying with the wrist-rest of the black catapult. It crossed my mind that my father looked worried, but he was good at acting and perhaps that was just what he wanted me to think, so deep down I remained unconvinced.

'I suppose I'd better tell you,' he said, then turned away again, taking up a wooden spoon and stirring the soup. I waited. 'It's Eric.'

Then I knew what had happened. He didn't have to tell me the rest. I suppose I could have thought from the little he'd said up until then that my half-brother was dead, or ill, or that something had happened *to* him, but I knew then it was something Eric had done, and there was only one thing he could have done which would make my father look worried. He had escaped. I didn't say anything, though.

'Eric has escaped from the hospital. That was what Diggs came to tell us. They think he might head back here. Take those things off the table; I've told you before.' He sipped the soup, his back still turned. I waited until he started to turn round, then took the catapult, binoculars and spade off the table. In the same flat tone my father went on; 'Well, I don't suppose he'll get this far. They'll probably pick him up in a day or two. I just thought I'd tell you. In case anybody else hears and says anything. Get out a plate.'

I went to the cupboard and took out a plate, then sat down again, one leg crossed underneath me. My father went back to stirring the soup, which I could smell now above the cigar smoke. I could feel excitement in my stomach – a rising, tingling rush. So Eric was coming back home again; that was good-bad. I knew he'd make it. I didn't even think of asking the Factory about it; he'd be here. I wondered how long it would take him, and whether Diggs would now have to go shouting through the town, warning that the mad boy who *set fire to dogs* was on the loose again; lock up your hounds!

My father ladled some soup into my plate. I blew on it. I thought of the Sacrifice Poles. They were my early-warning system and deterrent rolled into one; infected, potent things which looked out from the island, warding off. Those totems were my warning shot; anybody who set foot on the island after seeing them should know what to expect. But it looked like, instead of being a clenched and threatening fist, they would present a welcoming, open hand. For Eric.

'I see you washed your hands again,' my father said as I sipped the hot soup. He was being sarcastic. He took the bottle of whisky from the dresser and poured himself a drink. The other glass, which I guessed had been the constable's, he put in the sink. He sat down at the far end of the table.

My father is tall and slim, though slightly stooped. He has a delicate face, like a woman's, and his eyes are dark. He limps now, and has done ever since I can remember. His left leg is almost totally stiff, and he usually takes a stick with him when he leaves the house. Some days, when it's damp, he has to use the stick inside, too, and I can hear him clacking about the uncarpeted rooms and corridors of the house; a hollow noise, going from place to place. Only here in the kitchen is the stick quieted; the flagstones silence it.

That stick is the symbol of the Factory's security. My father's leg, locked solid, has given me my sanctuary up in the warm space of the big loft, right at the top of the house where the junk and the rubbish are, where the dust moves and the sunlight slants and the Factory sits – silent, living and still.

My father can't climb up the narrow ladder from the top floor; and, even if he could, I know he wouldn't be able to negotiate the twist you have to make to get from the top of the ladder, round the brickwork of the chimney flues, and into the loft proper.

So the place is mine.

I suppose my father is about forty-five now, though sometimes I think he looks a lot older, and occasionally I think he might be a little younger. He won't tell me his real age, so forty-five is my estimate, judging by his looks.

'What height is this table?' he said suddenly, just as I was about to go to the breadbin for a slice to wipe my plate with. I turned round and looked at him, wondering why he was bothering with such an easy question.

'Thirty inches,' I told him, and took a crust from the bin.

'Wrong,' he said with an eager grin. 'Two foot six.'

I shook my head at him, scowling, and wiped the brown rim of soup from the inside of my plate. There was a time when I was genuinely afraid of these idiotic questions, but now, apart from the fact that I must know the height, length, breadth, area and volume of just about every part of the house and everything in it, I can see my father's obsession for what it is. It gets embarrassing at times when there are guests in the house, even if they are family and ought to know what to expect. They'll be sitting there, probably in the lounge, wondering whether Father's going to feed them anything or just give an impromptu lecture on cancer of the colon or tapeworms, when he'll sidle up to somebody, look round to make sure everybody's watching, then in a conspiratorial stage-whisper say: 'See that door over there? It's eighty-five inches, corner to corner.' Then he'll wink and walk off, or slide over on his seat, looking nonchalant.

Ever since I can remember there have been little stickers of white paper all over the house with neat black-biro writing on them. Attached to the legs of chairs, the edges of rugs, the bottoms of jugs, the aerials of radios, the doors of drawers, the headboards of beds, the screens of televisions, the handles of pots and pans, they give the appropriate measurement for the part of the object they're stuck to. There are even ones in pencil stuck to the leaves of plants. When I was a child I once went round the house tearing all the stickers off; I was belted and sent to my room for two days. Later my father decided it would be useful and character-forming for me to know all the

11

measurements as well as he did, so I had to sit for hours with the Measurement Book (a huge loose-leaf thing with all the information on the little stickers carefully recorded according to room and category of object), or go round the house with a jotter, making my own notes. This was all in addition to the usual lessons my father gave me on mathematics and history and so on. It didn't leave much time for going out to play, and I resented it a great deal. I was having a War at the time – the Mussels against the Dead Flies I think it was – and while I was in the library poring over the book and trying to keep my eyes open, soaking up all those damn silly Imperial measurements, the wind would be blowing my fly armies over half the island and the sea would first sink the mussel shells in their high pools and then cover them with sand. Luckily my father grew tired of this grand scheme and contented himself with firing the odd surprise question at me concerning the capacity of the umbrella-stand in pints or the total area in fractions of an acre of all the curtains in the house actually hung up at the time.

'I'm not answering these questions any more,' I said to him as I took my plate to the sink. 'We should have gone metric years ago.'

My father snorted into his glass as he drained it. 'Hectares and that sort of rubbish. Certainly not. It's all based on the measurement of the globe, you know. I don't have to tell you what nonsense *that* is.'

I sighed as I took an apple from the bowl on the window sill. My father once had me believing that the earth was a Möbius strip, not a sphere. He still maintains that he believes this, and makes a great show of sending off a manuscript to publishers down in London, trying to get them to publish a book expounding this view, but I know he's just mischief-making again, and gets most of his pleasure from his acts of stunned disbelief and then righteous indignation when the manuscript is eventually returned. This occurs about every three months, and I doubt that life would be half as much fun for him without this sort of ritual. Anyway, that is one of his reasons for not switching over to a metric standard for his stupid measurements, though in fact he's just lazy.

'What were you up to today?' He stared across the table at

12

me, rolling the empty tumbler around on the wooden table-top.

I shrugged. 'Out. Walking and things.'

'Building dams again?' he sneered.

'No,' I said, shaking my head confidently and biting the apple. 'Not today.'

'I hope you weren't out killing any of God's creatures.'

I shrugged at him again. Of course I was out killing things. How the hell am I supposed to get heads and bodies for the Poles and the Bunker if I don't kill things? There just aren't enough natural deaths. You can't explain that sort of thing to people, though.

'Sometimes I think you're the one who should be in hospital, not Eric.' He was looking at me from under his dark brows, his voice low. Once, that sort of talk would have scared me, but not now. I'm nearly seventeen, and not a child. Here in Scotland I'm old enough to get married without my parent's permission, and have been for a year. There wouldn't be much point to me getting married perhaps – I'll admit that – but the principle is there.

Besides, I'm not Eric; I'm me and I'm here and that's all there is to it. I don't bother people and they had best not bother me if they know what's good for them. *I* don't go giving people presents of burning dogs, or frighten the local toddlers with handfuls of maggots and mouthfuls of worms. The people in the town may say 'Oh, he's not all there, you know,' but that's just their little joke (and sometimes, just to rub it in, they don't point to their heads as they say it); I don't mind. I've learned to live with my disability, and learned to live without other people, so it's no skin off my nose.

My father seemed to be trying to hurt me, though; he wouldn't say something like that normally. The news about Eric must have shaken him. I think he knew, just as I did, that Eric would get back, and he was worried about what would happen. I didn't blame him, and I didn't doubt that he was also worried about me. I represent a crime, and if Eric was to come back stirring things up The Truth About Frank might come out.

I was never registered. I have no birth certificate, no

13

National Insurance number, nothing to say I'm alive or have ever existed. I know this is a crime, and so does my father, and I think that sometimes he regrets the decision he made seventeen years ago, in his hippy–anarchist days, or whatever they were.

Not that I've suffered, really. I enjoyed it, and you could hardly say that I wasn't educated. I probably know more about the conventional school subjects than most people of my age. I could complain about the truth of *some* of the bits of information my father passed on to me, mind you. Ever since I was able to go into Porteneil alone and check things up in the library my father has had to be pretty straight with me, but when I was younger he used to fool me time after time, answering my honest if naïve questions with utter rubbish. For *years* I believed Pathos was one of the Three Musketeers, Fellatio was a character in *Hamlet*, Vitreous a town in China, and that the Irish peasants had to tread the peat to make Guinness.

Well, these days I can reach the highest shelves of the house library, and walk into Porteneil to visit the one there, so I can check up on anything my father says, and he has to tell me the truth. It annoys him a lot, I think, but that's the way things go. Call it progress.

But I am educated. While he wasn't able to resist indulging his rather immature sense of humour by selling me a few dummies, my father couldn't abide a son of his not being a credit to him in some way; my body was a forlorn hope for any improvement, so only my mind was left. Hence all my lessons. My father is an educated man, and he passed a lot of what he already knew on to me, as well as doing a fair bit of study himself into areas he didn't know all that much about just so that he could teach me. My father is a doctor of chemistry, or perhaps biochemistry – I'm not sure. He seems to have known enough about ordinary medicine – and perhaps still have had the contacts within the profession – to make sure that I got my inoculations and injections at the correct times in my life, despite my official non-existence as far as the National Health Service is concerned.

I think my father used to work in a university for a few years after he graduated, and he might have invented something; he occasionally hints that he gets some sort of royalty from a patent or something, but I suspect the old hippy survives on whatever family wealth the Cauldhames still have secreted away.

The family has been in this part of Scotland for about two hundred years or more, from what I can gather, and we used to own a lot of the land around here. Now all we have is the island, and that's pretty small, and hardly even an island at low tide. The only other remnant of our glorious past is the name of Porteneil's hot-spot, a grubby old pub called the Cauldhame Arms where I go sometimes now, though still under age of course, and watch some of the local youths trying to be punk bands. That was where I met and still meet the only person I'd call a friend; Jamie the dwarf, whom I let sit on my shoulders so he can see the bands.

'Well, I don't think he'll get this far. They'll pick him up,' my father said again, after a long and brooding silence. He got up to rinse his glass. I hummed to myself, something I always used to do when I wanted to smile or laugh, but thought the better of it. My father looked at me. 'I'm going to the study. Don't forget to lock up, all right?'

'Okey-doke,' I said, nodding.

'Goodnight.'

My father left the kitchen. I sat and looked at my trowel, Stoutstroke. Little grains of dry sand stuck to it, so I brushed them off. The study. One of my few remaining unsatisfied ambitions is to get into the old man's study. The cellar I have at least seen, and been in occasionally; I know all the rooms on the ground floor and the second; the loft is my domain entirely and home of the Wasp Factory, no less; but that one room on the first floor I don't know, I have never even seen inside.

I do know he has some chemicals in there, and I suppose he does experiments or something, but what the room looks like, what he actually does in there, I have no idea. All I've ever got out of it are a few funny smells and the tap-tap of my father's stick.

I stroked the long handle of the trowel, wondering if my

father had a name for that stick of his. I doubted it. He doesn't attach the same importance to them as I do. I know they are important.

I think there is a secret in the study. He had hinted as much more than once, just vaguely, just enough to entice me so that I want to ask what, so that he knows that I want to ask. I don't ask, of course, because I wouldn't get any worthwhile answer. If he did tell me anything it would be a pack of lies, because obviously the secret wouldn't be a secret any more if he told me the truth, and he can feel, as I do, that with my increasing maturity he needs all the holds over me he can get; I'm not a child any more. Only these little bits of bogus power enable him to think he is in control of what he sees as the correct father–son relationship. It's pathetic really, but with his little games and his secrets and his hurtful remarks he tries to keep his security intact.

I leaned back in the wooden chair and stretched. I like the smell of the kitchen. The food, and the mud on our wellingtons, and sometimes the faint tang of cordite coming up from the cellar all give me a good, tight, thrilling feel when I think about them. It smells different when it's been raining and our clothes are wet. In the winter the big black stove pumps out heat fragrant with driftwood or peat, and everything steams and the rain hammers against the glass. Then it has a comfortable, closed-in feeling, making you feel cosy, like a great big cat with its tail curled round itself. Sometimes I wish we had a cat. All I've ever had was a head, and that the seagulls took.

I went to the toilet, down the corridor off the kitchen, for a crap. I didn't need a pee because I'd been pissing on the Poles during the day, infecting them with my scent and power.

I sat there and thought about Eric, to whom such an unpleasant thing happened. Poor twisted bugger. I wondered, as I have often wondered, how I would have coped. But it didn't happen to me. I have stayed here and Eric was the one who went away and it all happened somewhere else, and that's all there is to it. I'm me and here's here.

I listened, wondering if I could hear my father. Perhaps he had gone straight to bed. He often sleeps in the study rather than in the big bedroom on the second floor, where mine is. Maybe that room holds too many unpleasant (or pleasant) memories for him. Either way, I couldn't hear any snoring.

I hate having to sit down in the toilet all the time. With my unfortunate disability I usually have to, as though I was a bloody woman, but I hate it. Sometimes in the Cauldhame Arms I stand up at the urinal, but most if it ends up running down my hands or legs.

I strained. Plop splash. Some water came up and hit my bum, and that was when the phone went.

'Shit,' I said, and then laughed at myself. I cleaned my arse quickly and pulled my trousers up, pulling the chain, too, and then waddling out into the corridor, zipping up. I ran up the broad stairs to the first-floor landing, where our only phone is. I'm forever on at my father to get more phones put in, but he says we don't get called often enough to warrant extensions. I got to the phone before whoever was calling rang off. My father hadn't appeared.

'Hello,' I said. It was a call-box.

'Skraw-*aak*!' screamed a voice at the other end. I held the receiver away from my ear and looked at it, scowling. Tinny yells continued to come from the earpiece. When they stopped I put my ear back to it.

'Porteneil 531,' I said coldly.

'Frank! Frank! It's me. Me! Hello there! Hello!'

'Is there an echo on this line or are you saying everything twice?' I said. I could recognise Eric's voice.

'Both! Ha ha ha ha ha!'

'Hello, Eric. Where are you?'

'Here! Where are you?'

'Here.'

'If we're both here, why are we bothering with the phone?'

'Tell me where you are before your money runs out.'

'But if you're *here* you must know. Don't you know where you are?' He started to giggle.

I said calmly: 'Stop being silly, Eric.'

'I'm not being silly. I'm not telling you where I am; you'll only tell Angus and he'll tell the police and they'll take me back to the fucking hospital.'

17

'Don't use four-letter words. You know I don't like them. Of course I won't tell Dad.'

'"Fucking" is not a four-letter word. It's . . . it's a seven-letter word. Isn't that your lucky number?'

'No. Look, will you tell me where you are? I want to know.'

'I'll tell you where I am if you'll tell me what your lucky number is.'

'My lucky number is *e*.'

'*That's* not a number. That's a letter.'

'It *is* a number. It's a transcendental number: 2.718—'

'That's cheating. I meant an integer.'

'You should have been more specific,' I said, then sighed as the pips sounded and Eric eventually put more money in. 'Do you want me to call you back?'

'Ho-ho. You aren't getting it out of me that easy. How are you, anyway?'

'I'm fine. How are you?'

'Mad, of course,' he said, quite indignantly. I had to smile.

'Look, I'm assuming you're coming back here. If you are, please don't burn any dogs or anything, OK?'

'What are you talking about? It's me. Eric. I don't burn dogs!' He started to shout. 'I don't burn fucking dogs! What the hell do you think I am? Don't accuse me of burning fucking dogs, you little bastard! *Bastard!*'

'All right, Eric, I'm sorry, I'm sorry,' I said as quickly as I could. 'I just want you to be OK; be careful. Don't do anything to antagonise people, you know? People can be awful sensitive. . . .'

'Well . . . ,' I could hear him say. I listened to him breathing, then his voice changed. 'Yeah, I'm coming back home. Just for a short while, to see how you both are. I suppose it's just you and the old man?'

'Yes, just the two of us. I'm looking forward to seeing you.'

'Oh, good.' There was a pause. 'Why don't you ever come to visit me?'

'I . . . I thought Father was down to see you at Christmas.'

'Was he? Well . . . but why don't *you* ever come?' He sounded plaintive. I shifted my weight on to my other foot, looked around the landing and up the stairs, half-expecting to see my father leaning over the banister rail, or to see his shadow on the wall of the landing above, where he thought he could hide and listen to my phone calls without me knowing.

'I don't like leaving the island for that long, Eric. I'm sorry, but I get this horrible feeling in my stomach, as though there's a great big knot in it. I just can't go that far away, not overnight or . . . I just can't. I want to see you, but you're so far away.'

'I'm getting closer.' He sounded confident again.

'Good. How far away are you?'

'Not telling you.'

'I told you my lucky number.'

'I lied. I'm still not going to tell you where I am.'

'That's not—'

'Well, I'll hang up now.'

'You don't want to talk to Dad?'

'Not yet. I'll talk to him later, when I'm a lot closer. I'm going now. See you. Take care.'

'*You* take care.'

'What's to worry about? I'll be all right. What can happen to me?'

'Just don't do anything to annoy people. You know; I mean, they get angry. About pets especially. I mean, I'm not—'

'What? *What?* What was that about pets?' he shouted.

'Nothing! I was just saying—'

'You little shit!' he screamed. 'You're accusing me of burning dogs again, aren't you? And I suppose I stick worms and maggots into kids' mouths and piss on them, too, eh?' he shrieked.

'Well,' I said carefully, toying with the flex, 'now you mention it—'

'Bastard! *Bastard!* You little shit! I'll kill you! You—' His voice disappeared, and I had to put the phone away from my ear again as he started to hammer the handset against the walls of the call-box. The succession of loud clunks sounded over the calm pips as his money ran out. I put the phone back in the cradle.

I looked up, but there was still no sign of Father. I crept up

19

the stairs and stuck my head between the banisters, but the landing was empty. I sighed and sat down on the stairs. I got the feeling I hadn't handled Eric very well over the phone. I'm not very good with people and, even though Eric is my brother, I haven't seen him for over two years, since he went crazy.

I got up and went back down to the kitchen to lock up and get my gear, then I went to the bathroom. I decided to watch the television in my room, or listen to the radio, and get to sleep early so I could be up just after dawn to catch a wasp for the Factory.

I lay on my bed listening to John Peel on the radio and the noise of the wind round the house and the surf on the beach. Beneath my bed my home-brew gave off a yeasty smell.

I thought again of the Sacrifice Poles; more deliberately this time, picturing each one in turn, remembering their positions and their components, seeing in my mind what those sightless eyes looked out to, and flicking through each view like a security guard changing cameras on a monitor screen. I felt nothing amiss; all seemed well. My dead sentries, those extensions of me which came under my power through the simple but ultimate surrender of death, sensed nothing to harm me or the island.

I opened my eyes and put the bedside light back on. I looked at myself in the mirror on the dressing-table over on the other side of the room. I was lying on top of the bed-covers, naked apart from my underpants.

I'm too fat. It isn't that bad, and it isn't my fault – but, all the same, I don't look the way I'd like to look. Chubby, that's me. Strong and fit, but still too plump. I want to look dark and menacing; the way I ought to look, the way I should look, the way I might have looked if I hadn't had my little accident. Looking at me, you'd never guess I'd killed three people. It isn't fair.

I switched the light out again. The room was totally dark, not even the starlight showing while my eyes adjusted. Perhaps I would ask for one of those LED alarm radios, though I'm very fond of my old brass alarm clock. Once I tied a wasp to the striking-surface of each of the copper-coloured bells on the top, where the little hammer would hit them in the morning when the alarm went off.

I always wake up before the alarm goes, so I got to watch.

2: The Snake Park

I TOOK the little cinder that was the remains of the wasp and put it into a matchbox, wrapped in an old photograph of Eric with my father. In the picture my father was holding a portrait-sized photograph of his first wife, Eric's mother, and she was the only one who was smiling. My father was staring at the camera looking morose. The young Eric was looking away and picking his nose, looking bored.

The morning was fresh and cold. I could see mist over the forests below the mountains, and fog out over the North Sea. I ran hard and fast along the wet sand where it was good and firm, making a jet noise with my mouth and holding my binoculars and bag down tight to my sides. When I got level with the Bunker I banked inland, slowing as I hit the soft white sand further up the beach. I checked the flotsam and jetsam as I swept over it, but there was nothing interesting-looking, nothing worth salvaging, just an old jelly-fish, a purple mass with four pale rings inside. I altered

22

course slightly to overfly it, going 'Trrrrrfffaow! Trrrrrrrrrrrrrrfffaow!' and kicking it on the run, blasting a dirty fountain of sand and jelly up and around me. '*Puchrrt*!' went the noise of the explosion. I banked again and headed for the Bunker.

The Poles were in good repair. I didn't need the bag of heads and bodies. I visited them all, working through the morning, planting the dead wasp in its paper coffin not between two of the more important Poles, as I had intended originally, but under the path, just on the island side of the bridge. While I was there I climbed up the suspension cables to the top of the mainland tower and looked around. I could see the top of the house and one of the skylights over the loft. I could also see the spire of the Church of Scotland in Porteneil, and some smoke coming up from the town chimneys. I took the small knife from my left breast pocket and nicked my left thumb carefully. I smeared the red stuff over the top of the main beam which crosses from one I-girder to the other on the tower, then wiped my small wound with an antiseptic tissue from one of my bags. I scrambled back down after that and retrieved the ball-bearing I had hit the sign with the day before.

The first Mrs Cauldhame, Mary, who was Eric's mother, died in childbirth in the house. Eric's head was too big for her; she haemorrhaged and bled to death on the marital bed back in 1960. Eric has suffered from quite severe migraine all his life, and I am very much inclined to attribute the ailment to his manner of entry into the world. The whole thing about his migraine and his dead mother had, I think, a lot to do with What Happened To Eric. Poor unlucky soul; he was just in the wrong place at the wrong time, and something very unlikely happened which by sheer chance mattered more to him than anybody else it could have happened to. But that's what you risk when you leave here.

Thinking about it, that means that Eric has killed somebody, too. I had thought that I was the only murderer in the family, but old Eric beat me to it, killing his mum before he had even drawn breath. Unintentional, admittedly, but it isn't always the thought that counts.

The Factory said something about fire.

I was still thinking about that, wondering what it really meant. The obvious interpretation was that Eric was going to set fire to some dogs, but I was too wise in the ways of the Factory to treat that as definite; I suspected there was more to it.

In a way, I was sorry Eric was coming back. I had been thinking of having a War shortly, maybe in the next week or so, but with Eric probably going to make an appearance I had decided against it. I hadn't had a good War for months; the last one had been the Ordinary Soldiers versus the Aerosols. In that scenario, all the 72nd-scale armies, complete with their tanks and guns and trucks and stores and helicopters and boats, had to unite against the Aerosol Invasion. The Aerosols were almost impossible to stop, and the soldiers and their weapons and equipment were getting burned and melted all over the place until one brave soldier who had clung on to one of the Aerosols as it flew back to its base came back (after many adventures) with the news that their base was a breadboard moored under an overhang on an inland creek. A combined force of commandos got there just in time and blew the base to smithereens, finally blowing up the overhang on top of the smoking remains. A good War, with all the right ingredients and a more spectacular ending than most (I even had my father asking me what all the explosions and the fire had been about, when I got back to the house that evening), but too long ago.

Anyway, with Eric on his way, I didn't think it would be a good idea to start another War only to have to abandon it in the middle of things and start dealing with the real world. I decided I would postpone hostilities for a while. Instead, after I had anointed a few of the more important Poles with precious substances, I built a dam system.

When I was younger I used to have fantasies about saving the house by building a dam. There would be a fire in the grass on the dunes, or a plane would have crashed, and all that stopped the cordite in the cellar from going up would be me diverting some of the water from a dam system down a channel

24

and into the house. At one time my major ambition was to have my father buy me an excavator so that I could make *really* big dams. But I have a far more sophisticated, even metaphysical, approach to dam-building now. I realise that you can never really win against the water; it will always triumph in the end, seeping and soaking and building up and undermining and overflowing. All you can really do is construct something that will divert it or block its way for a while; persuade it to do something it doesn't really want to do. The pleasure comes from the elegance of the compromise you strike between where the water wants to go (guided by gravity and the medium it's moving over) and what you want to do with it.

Actually, I think that life has few pleasures to compare with dam-building. Give me a good broad beach with a reasonable slope and not too much seaweed, and a fair-sized stream, and I'll be happy all day, any day.

By that time the sun was well up, and I took off my jacket to lay it with my bags and binoculars. Stoutstroke dipped and bit and sliced and dug, building a huge triple-deck dam, the main section of which backed up the water in the North Burn for eighty paces; not far off the record for the position I had chosen. I used my usual metal overflow piece, which I keep hidden in the dunes near the best dam-building site, and the *pièce de résistance* was an aqueduct bottomed with an old black plastic rubbish-bag I'd found in the driftwood. The aqueduct carried the overflow stream over three sections of a by-pass channel I'd cut from further up the dam. I built a little village downstream from the dam, complete with roads and a bridge over the remnant of the burn, and a church.

Bursting a good big dam, or even just letting it overflow, is almost as satisfying as planning and building it in the first place. I used little shells to represent the people in the town, as usual. Also as usual, none of the shells survived the flood when the dam burst; they all sank, which meant that everybody died.

By that time I was very hungry, my arms were getting sore and my hands were red with gripping the spade and digging into the sand by themselves. I watched the first flood of water race down to the sea, muddy and littered, then turned to head for home.

'Did I hear you talking on the phone last night?' my father said.

I shook my head. 'Nope.'

We were finishing our lunch, sitting in the kitchen, me with my stew, my father with brown rice and seaweed salad. He had his Town Gear on; brown brogues, brown tweed three-piece suit, and on the table sat his brown cap. I checked my watch and saw that it was Thursday. It was very unusual for him to go anywhere on a Thursday, whether Porteneil or any further afield. I wasn't going to ask him where he was going because he'd only lie. When I used to ask him where he was going he would tell me 'To Phucke', which he claimed was a small town to the north of Inverness. It was years and a lot of funny looks in the town before I learned the truth.

'I'm going out today,' he told me between mouthfuls of rice and salad. I nodded, and he continued: 'I'll be back late.'

Perhaps he was going to Porteneil to get drunk in the Rock Hotel, or perhaps he was off to Inverness, where he often goes on business he prefers to keep mysterious, but I suspected that it was really something to do with Eric.

'Right,' I said.

'I'll take a key, so you can lock up when you want to.' He clattered his knife and fork down on the empty plate and wiped his mouth on a brown napkin made from recycled paper. 'Just don't put all the bolts on, all right?'

'Right.'

'You'll make youself something to eat this evening, h'm?'

I nodded again, not looking up as I ate.

'And you'll do the washing-up?'

I nodded again.

'I don't think Diggs'll come round again; but, if he does, I want you to stay out of his way.'

'Don't worry,' I told him, and sighed.

'You'll be all right, then?' he said, standing.

'M'm-h'm,' I said, cleaning up the last of the stew.

'I'll be off, then.'

26

I looked up in time to see him place his cap on his head and look round the kitchen, patting his pockets as he did so. He looked at me again and nodded.

I said: 'Goodbye.'

'Yes,' he said. 'Right you are.'

'I'll see you later.'

'Yes.' He turned round, then turned back, looked once more round the room, then shook his head quickly and went to the door, taking his stick from the corner by the washing machine on his way out. I heard the outer door slam, then silence. I sighed.

I waited a minute or so then got up, leaving my almost clean plate, and went through the house to the lounge, where I could see the path leading away through the dunes towards the bridge. My father was walking along it, head bowed, going quickly with a sort of anxious swagger as he swung the stick. As I watched, he struck out with it at some wild flowers growing by the path-side.

I ran upstairs, pausing by the back stairwell window to watch my father disappear round the dune before the bridge, ran up the stairs, got to the door to the study and twisted the handle briskly. The door was firm; it didn't shift a millimetre. One day he'd forget, I was sure, but not today.

After I had finished my meal and done the washing-up, I went to my room, checked the home-brew and got my air-rifle. I made sure I had sufficient pellets in my jacket pockets, then headed out of the house for the Rabbit Grounds on the mainland, between the large branch of the creek and the town dump.

I don't like using the gun; it's almost too accurate for me. The catapult is an Inside thing, requiring that you and it are one. If you're feeling bad, you'll miss; or, if you know you're doing something wrong, you'll miss, too. Unless you fire a gun from the hip it's all Outside; you point and aim and that's it, unless the sights are out or there's a really high wind. Once you've cocked the gun the power's all there, just waiting to be released by the squeeze of a finger. A catapult lives with you until the last moment; it stays tensed in your hands, breathing

27

with you, moving with you, ready to leap, ready to sing and jerk, and leaving you in that dramatic pose, arms and hands outstretched while you wait for the dark curve of the ball in its flight to find its target, that delicious thud.

But going after rabbits, especially the cunning little bastards out on the Grounds, you need all the help you can get. One shot and they're scurrying for their holes. The gun is loud enough to frighten them just as much; but, calm, surgical thing that it is, it improves your chance of a first-time kill.

As far as I know, none of my ill-starred relations has ever died by the gun. They've gone a lot of funny ways, the Cauldhames and their associates by marriage, but to the best of my knowledge a gun has never crossed one off.

I came to the end of the bridge, where technically my territory stops, and stood still for a while, thinking, feeling, listening and looking and smelling. Everything seemed to be all right.

Quite apart from the ones I killed (and they were all about the same age I was when I murdered them) I can think of at least three of our family who went to whatever they imagined their Maker was like in unusual ways. Leviticus Cauldhame, my father's eldest brother, emigrated to South Africa and bought a farm there in 1954. Leviticus, a person of such weapon-grade stupidity his mental faculties would probably have improved with the onset of senile dementia, left Scotland because the Conservatives had failed to reverse the Socialist reforms of the previous Labour government: railways still nationalised; working class breeding like flies now the welfare state existed to prevent the natural culling by disease; state-owned mines . . . intolerable. I have read some of the letters he wrote to my father. Leviticus was happy with the country, though there were rather a lot of blacks around. He referred to the policy of separate development as 'apart-hate' in his first few letters, until somebody must have clued him in on the correct spelling. Not my father, I'm sure.

Leviticus was passing police headquarters in Johannesburg one day, walking along the pavement after a shopping expedition, when a crazed, homicidal black threw himself, unconscious, from the top storey and apparently ripped all his fingernails out on the way down. He hit and fatally injured my innocent and unfortunate uncle whose muttered last words in hospital, before his coma became a full stop, were: 'My God, the buggers've learned to fly. . . .'

A faint wisp of smoke rose ahead of me from the town dump. I wasn't going that far today, but I could hear the bulldozer they used sometimes to spread the garbage around as it revved and pushed.

I hadn't been to the dump for a while, and it was about time I went to see what the good folk of Porteneil had thrown out. That was where I got all the old aerosols for the last War, not to mention several important parts of the Wasp Factory, including the Face itself.

My uncle Athelwald Trapley, from my mother's side of the family, emigrated to America at the end of the Second World War. He threw in a good job with an insurance company to go off with a woman and ended up, broke and heartbroke, in a cheap caravan site outside Fort Worth, where he decided to put an end to himself.

He turned on his Calor-gas stove and heater but didn't light them and sat down to await the end. Understandably nervous, and no doubt a little distracted and distraught both with his loved one's untimely departure and that which he was planning for himself, he resorted without a thought to his habitual method of calming himself down, and lit a Marlboro.

Out of the blazing wreck he leaped, stumbling around on fire from head to toe and screaming. He had intended a painless death; not being burned alive. So he jumped head first into the forty-gallon oil-drum full of rainwater which stood at the rear of the caravan. Wedged inside that drum he drowned, his little legs waggling pathetically as he gulped and squirmed and tried to get his arms into a position from which he could lever himself out.

Twenty metres or so from the grass-packed hill which looks over the Rabbit Grounds I switched to Silent Running, pacing stealthily through the long weeds and reeds, careful not to let anything I was carrying make a noise. I was hoping to catch some of the little pests out early but, if I had to, I was prepared to wait until the sun went down.

29

I crawled quietly up the slope, the grass sliding under my chest and belly, my legs straining to propel my bulk up and forward. I was down-wind, of course, and the breeze was stiff enough to cover most small noises. As far as I could see, there were no rabbit sentries on the hill. I stopped about two metres down from the summit and quietly cocked the gun, inspecting the composite steel and nylon pellet before placing it in the chamber and snicking the gun closed. I closed my eyes and thought about the trapped, compressed spring and the little slug sitting at the shiny bottom of the rifled tube. Then I crawled to the top of the hill.

At first I thought I would have to wait. The Grounds looked empty in the afternoon light, and only the grass moved in the wind. I could see the holes and the little piles and scatters of droppings, and I could see the gorse bushes on the far slope above the bank which held most of the holes, where the rabbit-runs snaked tiny paths like jagged tunnels through the bushes, but there was no sign of the animals themselves. It was in those rabbit-runs through the gorse that some of the local boys used to set snares. I found the wire loops, though, having seen the boys set them, and I tore them out or put them under the grass on the paths the boys used to take when they came to inspect their traps. Whether any of them was tripped up by his own snare or not I don't know, but I'd like to think they did go sprawling head first. Anyway, they or their replacements don't set snares any more; I suppose it has gone out of fashion and they are out spraying slogans on walls, sniffing glue or trying to get laid.

Animals rarely surprise me but there was something about the buck, once I noticed it sitting there, that froze me for a second. It must have been there all the time, sitting motionless and staring straight at me from the far edge of the level area of the Grounds, but I hadn't noticed it at first. When I did, something about its stillness stilled me for a moment. Without actually moving physically, I shook my head clear inside and decided that the big male would make a fine head for a Pole. The rabbit might as well have been stuffed for all the movement it made, and I could see that it definitely was staring right at me, its little eyes not blinking, its tiny nose not

30

sniffing, its ears untwitched. I stared straight back at it and very slowly brought the gun round to bear, moving it first one way then slightly the other, so that it looked like something swaying with the wind in the grass. It took about a minute to get the rifle in place and my head in the correct position, cheek by stock, and still the beast hadn't moved a millimetre.

Four times larger, his big whiskered head split neatly into four by the crosshairs, he looked even more impressive, and just as immobile. I frowned and brought my head up, suddenly thinking that it might just *be* stuffed; perhaps somebody was having a laugh at my expense. Town boys? My father? Surely not Eric yet? It was a stupid thing to have done; I'd moved my head far too quickly for it to look natural, and the buck shot off up the bank. I dipped my head and brought the gun up at the same time without thinking. There was no time to get back into the right position, take a breath and gently squeeze the trigger; it was up and bang, and with my whole body unbalanced and both hands on the gun I fell forward, rolling as I did so to keep the gun out the sand.

When I looked up, cradling the gun and gasping, my backside sunk in sand, I couldn't see the rabbit. I forced the gun down and hit myself on the knees. 'Shit!' I told myself.

The buck wasn't in a hole, however. It wasn't even near the bank where the holes were. It was tearing across the level ground in great leaps, heading right at me and seeming to shake and shiver in mid-air with every bound. It was coming at me like a bullet, head shaking, lips curled back, teeth long and yellow and by far the biggest I'd ever seen on a rabbit, live or dead. Its eyes looked like coiled slugs. Blobs of red arced from its left haunch with every pouncing leap; it was almost on me, and I was sat there staring.

There was no time to reload. By the time I started to react there was no time to do anything except at the instinctive level. My hands left the gun hanging in mid-air above my knees and went for the catapult, which as always was hanging on my belt, the arm-rest stuck down between that and my cords. Even my quick-reaction steelies were beyond reach in time, though; the rabbit was on me in a half-second, heading straight for my throat.

I caught it with the catapult, the thick black tubing of the rubber twisting once in the air as I scissored my hands and fell back, letting the buck go over my head and then kicking with my legs and turning myself so that I was level with it where it lay, kicking and struggling with the power of a wolverine, spreadeagled on the sand slope with its neck caught in the black rubber. Its head twisted this way and that as it tried to reach my fingers with its chopping teeth. I hissed through my own teeth at it and tugged the rubber tighter, then tighter still. The buck thrashed and spat and made a high keening noise I didn't think rabbits were capable of and beat its legs on the ground. I was so rattled I glanced round to make sure this wasn't a signal for an army of bunnies like this Dobermann of a beast to come up from behind and tear me to shreds.

The damn thing wouldn't die! The rubber was stretching and stretching and not tightening enough, and I couldn't move my hands for fear of it tearing the flesh off a finger or biting my nose off. The same consideration stopped me from butting the animal; I wasn't going to put my face near those teeth. I couldn't get a knee up to break its back, either, because I was almost slipping down the slope as it was, and I couldn't possibly get any purchase on that surface with only one leg. It was crazy! This wasn't Africa! It was a rabbit, not a lion! What the hell was happening here?

It finally bit me, twisting its neck more than I would have thought possible and catching my right index finger right on the knuckle.

That was it. I screamed and pulled with all my might, shaking my hands and my head and throwing myself backwards and over as I did so, banging one knee off the gun where it lay, fallen in the sand.

I ended up lying in the scrubby grass at the bottom of the hill, my knuckles white as I throttled the rabbit, swinging it in front of my face with its neck held on the thin black line of rubber tubing, now tied like a knot on a black string. I was still shaking, so I couldn't tell if the vibrations the body made were its or mine. Then the tubing gave way. The rabbit slammed into my left hand while the other end of the rubber whipped my right wrist; my arms flew out in opposite directions, crashing into the ground.

I lay on my back, my head on the sandy ground, staring out to the side where the body of the buck lay at the end of a little curved line of black, and tangled in the arm-rest and grip of the catapult. The animal was still.

I looked up at the sky and made a fist with the other hand, beating it into the ground. I looked back at the rabbit, then got up and knelt over it. It was dead; the head rolled slack, neck broken, when I lifted it. The left haunch was matted red with blood where my pellet had hit it. It was big; size of a tomcat; the biggest rabbit I'd ever seen. Obviously I'd left the rabbits alone for too long, or I'd have known about the existence of such a brute.

I sucked at the little trickle of blood from my finger. My catapult, my pride and joy, the Black Destroyer, itself destroyed by a *rabbit!* Oh, I suppose I could have written off and got a new length of rubber, or got old Cameron in the ironmonger's shop to find me something, but it would never feel right again. Every time I lifted it to aim it at a target – living or not – this moment would be at the back of my mind. The Black Destroyer was finished.

I sat back in the sand and looked quickly round the area. Still no other rabbits. Hardly surprising. There was no time to waste. There's only one way to react after something like this.

I got up, retrieved the rifle, lying half-buried in the sand on the slope, went to the top of the hill, looked round, then decided to risk leaving everything as it was. I cradled the gun in my arms and set off at Emergency Speed, hurtling down the path back to the island at maximum, trusting to luck and adrenalin that I wouldn't put a foot wrong and end up lying gasping in the grass with a multiple fracture of the femur. I used the gun to balance myself with on the tighter corners; the grass and the ground were both dry, so it wasn't as risky as it might have been. I cut off the path proper and charged up over a dune and down its other side to where the service pipe carrying the water and electricity to the house appears out of the sand and crosses the creek. I jumped the iron spikes and landed with both feet on the concrete, then ran over the narrow top of the pipe and jumped down on to the island.

Back at the house I went straight to my shed. I left the rifle, checked the War Bag and put its strap over my head, tying the waist-string quickly. I locked the shed again and jogged as far as the bridge while I got my breath back. Once through the narrow gate in the middle of the bridge I sprinted.

At the Rabbit Grounds, everything was as I'd left it – the buck lying strangled in the broken catapult, the sand kicked up and messed where I'd gone crashing. The wind still moved the grass and flowers, and there were no animals around; even the gulls hadn't spotted the carrion yet. I got straight to work.

First I took a twenty-centimetre electric-piping bomb out of the War Bag. I slit the buck in the anus. I checked that the bomb was all right, especially that the white crystals of the explosive mixture were dry, then added a plastic-straw fuse and a charge of the explosive around the hole bored in the black pipe and taped everything up. I shoved the lot inside the still warm rabbit and left it sort of sitting, squatting looking towards the holes in the bank. Then I took some smaller bombs and planted them inside some of the rabbit holes, stamping down the roofs of the tunnel entrances so that they caved in and left only the straw fuses sticking out. I filled the plastic detergent-bottle and primed the lighter, left it lying on the top of the bank most of the rabbit holes were in, then went back to the first of the blocked-up holes and lit the fuse with my disposable cigarette-lighter. The smell of burning plastic stayed in my nose and the bright glare of the burning mixture danced in my eyes as I hurried to the next hole, glancing at my watch as I did so. I'd placed six smaller bombs, and had them all lit in forty seconds.

I was sitting on the top of the bank, above the holes, the lighter of the Flame-thrower burning weakly in the sunlight, when, just over the minute, the first tunnel blew. I felt it through the seat of my pants, and grinned. The rest went off quickly, the puff of smoke from the charge around the mouth of each bomb bursting out of the fuming earth just before the main charge went off. Scattering earth was blasted out into the Rabbit Grounds, and the thudding noises rolled through the air. I smiled at that. There was very little noise really. You wouldn't have been able to hear a thing back at the house.

Almost all the energy from the bombs had gone into blowing the earth out and the air in the burrows back.

The first dazed rabbits came out; two of them bleeding at the nose, looking otherwise unharmed but staggering, almost falling. I squeezed the plastic bottle and sent a jet of petrol out of it, over the wick of the lighter, held a few centimetres out from the nozzle by an aluminium tent-peg. The petrol burst into flame as it flew over the wick in the tiny steel cup, roared through the air and fell brightly on and around the two rabbits. They took flame and blazed, running and stumbling and falling. I looked round for more as the first two flamed near the centre of the Grounds, finally collapsing into the grass, stiff-limbed but twitching, crackling to the breeze. A tiny lick of flame flickered round the mouth of the 'thrower; I blew it out. Another, smaller rabbit appeared. I caught it with the jet of flame and it zipped off out of range, heading for the water by the side of the hill the savage buck had attacked me on. I dug into the War Bag, drew out the air-pistol, cocked it and fired in one movement. The shot missed and the rabbit trailed a thread of smoke round the hill.

I got another three rabbits with the 'thrower before I packed it in. The last thing I did was to fire the blazing stream of petrol at the buck still sitting stuffed and dead and oozing blood in the forefront of the Grounds. The fire dropped all round it so that it disappeared in the rolling orange and curling black. In a few seconds the fuse caught, and after about ten seconds the mass of flame blew up and out, throwing something black and smoking twenty metres or more into the late-afternoon air and scattering pieces all over the Grounds. The explosion, much bigger than the ones in the holes, and with almost nothing to muffle it, cracked across the dunes like a whip, setting my ears ringing and making even me jump a bit.

Whatever was left of the buck landed way behind me. I followed the smell of burning to where it lay. It was mostly the head, and a grubby stub of spine and ribs, and about half the skin. I gritted my teeth and picked the warm remnant up, took it back to the Grounds and flung it into them from the top of the bank.

I stood in the slanting sunlight, warm and yellow around me, the stench of burning flesh and grass on the wind, the smoke rising into the air from burrows and cadavers, grey and black, the sweet smell of leaking unburned petrol coming from the Flame-thrower where I'd left it, and I breathed deeply.

With the last of the petrol I covered the body of the catapult and the used-up bottle of the 'thrower where they lay on the sand and set fire to them. I sat cross-legged just by the blaze, staring into it from up-wind until it was out and only the metal of the Black Destroyer remained, then I took the sooty skeleton and buried it where it had been ruined, at the bottom of the hill. It would have a name now: Black Destroyer Hill.

The fire was out everywhere; the grass too young and moist to catch. Not that I'd have cared if it had gone up. I considered setting the whin bushes alight, but the flowers always looked cheerful when they came out, and the bushes smelled better fresh than burned, so I didn't. I decided I'd caused enough mayhem for one day. The catapult was avenged, the buck – or what it meant, its spirit maybe – soiled and degraded, taught a hard lesson, and I felt *good*. If the rifle was all right and hadn't got sand inside the sights or anywhere else awkward to clean, it would almost have been worth it. The Defence budget would stand buying another catapult tomorrow; my crossbow would just have to wait another week or so.

With that lovely sated feeling inside me, I packed the War Bag and went wearily home, thinking what had happened over in my mind, trying to figure out the whys and wherefores, see what lessons were to be learned, what signs to be read in it all.

On the way I passed the rabbit I thought had escaped, lying just before the sparkling clean water of the stream; blackened and contorted, locked into a weird, twisted crouch, its dead dry eyes staring up at me as I passed by, accusatory.

I kicked it into the water.

My other dead uncle was called Harmsworth Stove, a half-uncle from Eric's mother's side of the family. He was a businessman in Belfast, and he and his wife looked after Eric for nearly five years, when my brother was a toddler. Harmsworth committed suicide, eventually, with an electric power-drill and a quarter-inch bit. He inserted it through the side of his skull and, finding that he was still alive though in some pain, drove to a nearby hospital, where he later died. Actually, I might just have had a little to do with his death, as it occurred less than a year after the Stoves lost their only child, Esmerelda. Unknown to them – and to everybody else, for that matter – she was one of my victims.

I lay in bed that night, waiting for my father to return, and for the phone to ring, while I thought about what had happened. Maybe the big buck was a rabbit from outside the Grounds, some wild beast come into the warren from beyond, to terrorise the locals and make itself boss, only to die in an encounter with a superior being it could have no real comprehension of.

Whatever, it was a Sign. I was sure of that. The whole fraught episode must signify something. My automatic response might just have had something to do with the fire that the Factory had predicted, but deep inside I knew that that wasn't all there was to it, and that there was more to come. The sign was in the whole thing, not just the unexpected ferocity of the buck I'd killed, but also in my furious, almost unthinking response and the fate of the innocent rabbits who took the brunt of my wrath.

It also meant something looking back as well as forward. The first time I murdered it was because of rabbits meeting a fiery death, and meeting that fiery death from the nozzle of a Flame-thrower virtually identical to the one I had used to exact my revenge on the warren. It was all too much, all too close and perfect. Events were shaping up faster and worse than I could have expected. I was in danger of losing control of the situation. The Rabbit Grounds – that supposed happy hunting-ground – had shown it could happen.

From the smaller to the greater, the patterns always hold true, and the Factory has taught me to watch out for them and respect them.

That was the first time I killed, because of what my cousin Blyth Cauldhame had done to our rabbits, Eric's and mine. It was Eric who first invented the Flame-thrower, and it was lying in what was then the bicycle-shed (now my shed) when our cousin, who had come to spend the weekend with us along with his parents, decided it would be fun to ride Eric's bike into the soft mud at the south end of the island. This he duly did while Eric and I were out flying kites. Then he came back and filled the Flame-thrower with petrol. He sat in the back garden with it, obscured from the windows of the lounge (where his parents and our father sat) by the washing blowing in the breeze; he lit the 'thrower and sprayed our two hutches with flame, incinerating all our beauties.

Eric in particular was very upset. He cried like a girl. I wanted to kill Blyth there and then; the hiding he got from his father, my dad's brother James, was not enough as far as I was concerned, not for what he'd done to Eric, *my brother*. Eric was inconsolable, desperate with grief because he had made the thing Blyth had used to destroy our beloved pets. He always was a bit sentimental, always the sensitive one, the bright one; until his nasty experience everybody was sure he would go far. Anyway, that was the start of the Skull Grounds, the area of the big, old, partially earthed-over dune behind the house where all our pets went when they died. The burned rabbits started that. Old Saul was there before them, but that was just a one-off thing.

I hadn't said anything to anybody, even Eric, about what I wanted to do to Blyth. I was wise in my childishness even then, at the tender age of five, when most children are forever telling their parents and friends that they hate them and they wish they were dead. I kept quiet.

When Blyth came back the next year he was even more unpleasant than before, having lost his left leg from above the knee in a road accident (the boy he was playing 'chicken' with was killed). Blyth resented his handicap bitterly; he was ten by that time, and very active. He tried to pretend that the nasty pink thing he had to strap on didn't exist, that it had nothing to do with him. He could just about ride a bike and he liked wrestling and playing football, usually in goal. I was just six then, and while Blyth knew that I had had some sort of little accident when I was much younger I certainly seemed to him to be a lot more able-bodied that he was. He thought it

38

was great fun to throw me about and wrestle with me and punch and kick me. I made a convincing show of joining in all this horse-play and appeared to enjoy it hugely for a week or so while I thought about what I could do to our cousin.

My other brother, a full brother, Paul, was still alive at the time. He, Eric and I were supposed to keep Blyth entertained. We did our best, taking Blyth to our favourite places, letting him play with our toys, and playing games with him. Eric and I had to restrain him at times when he wanted to do something like throw little Paul into the water to see if he'd float, or like when he wanted to fell a tree over the railway line that goes through Porteneil, but as a rule we got on surprisingly well, even though it rankled to see Eric, who was the same age as Blyth, obviously in fear of him.

So one day, very hot and insecty, with a faint breeze coming in off the sea, we were all lying in the grass on the flat area just to the south of the house. Paul and Blyth had fallen asleep, and Eric was lying with his hands behind his neck, staring drowsily up at the bright blue. Blyth had taken off the hollow plastic leg and left it lying tangled in its straps and the long grass blades. I watched Eric fall slowly asleep, his head gently tipping to one side, eyes closing. I got up and went for a walk and ended up at the Bunker. It hadn't assumed the full importance it later would in my life, though I already liked the place and felt at home in its coolness and dark. It was an old concrete pillbox built just before the last war to house a gun covering the firth, and it stuck in the sand like a big grey tooth. I went inside and found the snake. It was an adder. I didn't see it for ages because I was too busy sticking an old rotten fence-post out through the slits in the pillbox, pretending it was a gun and firing at imaginary ships. It was only after I'd stopped doing that and gone into the corner to have a piss that I looked over into the other corner where there was a pile of rusty cans and old bottles; there I saw the jagged stripes of the sleeping snake.

I decided what I was going to do almost immediately. I went outside quietly and found a length of driftwood of the appropriate shape, came back to the Bunker, caught the snake by the neck with the piece of wood and bundled it into the first rusty can I could find which still had a lid.

I don't think the snake had fully wakened up when I caught it, and I was careful not to jar it as I ran back to where my brothers and Blyth were lying on the grass. Eric had rolled over and had one hand under his head, the other over his eyes. His mouth was open slightly and his chest moved slowly. Paul lay in the sunlight curled up into a little ball, quite still, and Blyth was lying on his stomach, hands under his cheek, the stump of his left leg drawn up in the flowers and the grass, sticking out from his shorts like some monstrous erection. I went closer, still clutching the rusty can in my shadow. The gable end of the house looked down on us from about fifty metres away, windowless. White sheets flapped feebly in the back garden. My heart beat wildly and I licked my lips.

I sat down by the side of Blyth, careful not to let my shadow cross his face. I put one ear to the can and held it still. I couldn't hear or feel the snake stir. I reached for Blyth's artificial leg, lying smooth and pink by the small of his back and in his shadow. I held the leg to the can and took the lid away, sliding the leg over the hole as I did so. Then I slowly turned the can and the leg the other way up, so that the can was over the leg. I shook the can, and felt the snake fall into the leg. It didn't like it at first, and moved and beat against the sides of the plastic and the neck of the can while I held it and sweated, listening to the hum of the insects and the rustling of the grass, staring at Blyth as he lay there still and silent, his dark hair ruffled now and again by the breeze. My hands shook and the perspiration ran into my eyes.

The snake stopped moving. I held it longer, glancing at the house again. Then I tipped the leg and the can over until the leg was lying at the same angle on the grass as it had been, behind Blyth. I took the can carefully away at the last moment. Nothing happened. The snake was still inside the leg, and I couldn't even see it. I got up, walked backwards towards the nearest dune, threw the can way high over the top of it, then came back, lay down where I'd been sitting earlier, and closed my eyes.

Eric woke first, then I opened my eyes as though sleepily, and we woke little Paul, and our cousin. Blyth saved me the

trouble of suggesting a game of football by doing it himself.
Eric, Paul and I got the goalposts together while Blyth
hurriedly strapped his leg on.

Nobody suspected. From the first moments, when my
brothers and I stood there incredulous as Blyth screamed and
jumped and tugged at his leg, to the tearful farewell of Blyth's
parents and Diggs taking statements (a bit even appeared in
the *Inverness Courier* which was picked up for its curiosity
value by a couple of the Fleet Street rags), not one person even
suggested that it might have been anything other than a tragic
and slightly macabre accident. Only I knew better.

I didn't tell Eric. He was shocked by what had happened
and genuinely sorry for Blyth and his parents. All I said was
that I thought it was a judgement from God that Blyth had
first lost his leg and then had the replacement become the
instrument of his downfall. All because of the rabbits. Eric,
who was going through a religious phase at the time which I
suppose I was to some extent copying, thought this was a
terrible thing to say; God wasn't like that. I said the one I
believed in was.

At any rate, such was the reason *that* particular patch of
ground got its name: the Snake Park.

I lay in bed, thinking back on all this. Father still hadn't come
back. Perhaps he was going to stay out all night. That was
extremely unusual, and rather worrying. Perhaps he had been
knocked down, or had died of a heart attack.

I've always had a rather ambivalent attitude towards
something happening to my father, and it persists. A death is
always exciting, always makes you realise how alive you are,
how vulnerable but so-far-lucky; but the death of somebody
close gives you a good excuse to go a bit crazy for a while and
do things that would otherwise be inexcusable. What delight
to behave really badly and still get loads of sympathy!

But I'd miss him, and I don't know what the legal position
would be about me staying on here by myself. Would I get all
his money? *That* would be good; I could get my motorbike
now instead of having to wait. Jesus, there'd be so many things

I could do I don't even know where to start thinking about them. But it would be a big change, and I don't know that I'm ready for it yet.

I could feel myself starting to slide off into sleep; I began to imagine and see all sorts of weird things behind my eyes: maze-shapes and spreading areas of unknown colours, then fantastic buildings and spaceships and weapons and land-scapes. I often wish I could remember my dreams better. . . .

Two years after I killed Blyth I murdered my young brother Paul, for quite different and more fundamental reasons than I'd disposed of Blyth, and then a year after that I did for my young cousin Esmerelda, more or less on a whim.

That's my score to date. Three. I haven't killed anybody for years, and don't intend to ever again.

It was just a stage I was going through.

3: In the Bunker

MY GREATEST ENEMIES are Women and the Sea. These things I hate. Women because they are weak and stupid and live in the shadow of men and are nothing compared to them, and the Sea because it has always frustrated me, destroying what I have built, washing away what I have left, wiping clean the marks I have made. And I'm not all that sure the Wind is blameless, either.

The Sea is a sort of mythological enemy, and I make what you might call sacrifices to it in my soul, fearing it a little, respecting it as you're supposed to, but in many ways treating it as an equal. It does things to the world, and so do I; we should both be feared. Women . . . well, women are a bit too close for comfort as far as I'm concerned. I don't even like having them on the island, not even Mrs Clamp, who comes every week on a Saturday to clean the house and deliver our supplies. She's ancient, and sexless the way the very old and the very young are, but she's still *been* a woman, and I resent that, for my own good reason.

I woke the next morning, wondering if my father had come back or not. Without bothering to dress, I went to his room. I was going to try the door, but I could hear him snoring before I touched the handle, so I turned and went to the bathroom.

In the bathroom, after a piss, I went through my daily washing ritual. First I had my shower. The shower is the only time in any twenty-four-hour period I take my underpants right off. I put the old pair in the dirty-linen bag in the airing cupboard. I showered carefully, starting at my hair and ending between my toes and under my toenails. Sometimes, when I have to make precious substances such as toenail cheese or belly-button fluff, I have to go without a shower or bath for days and days; I hate doing this because I soon feel dirty and itchy, and the only bright thing about such abstinence is how good it feels to have a shower at the end of it.

After my shower, and a brisk rub-down with first a face-cloth and then a towel, I trimmed my nails. Then I brushed my teeth thoroughly with my electric toothbrush. Next the shave. I always use shaving foam and the latest razors (twin-blade swivel-heads are state-of-the-art at the moment), removing the downy brown growth of the previous day and night with dexterity and precision. As with all my ablutions, the shave follows a definite and predetermined pattern; I take the same number of strokes of the same length in the same sequence each morning. As always, I felt a rising tingle of excitement as I contemplated the meticulously shorn surfaces of my face.

I blew and picked my nose clean, washed my hands, cleaned the razor, nail-clipper, shower and basin, rinsed out the flannel and combed my hair. Happily I didn't have any spots, so there was nothing else required but a final handwash and a clean pair of underpants. I placed all my washing materials, towels, razor and so forth exactly where they should be, wiped a little steam off the mirror on my bathroom cabinet, and returned to my room.

There I put on my socks; green for that day. Then a khaki shirt with pockets. In the winter I'd have a vest underneath

44

and a green army jumper over the shirt, but not in the summer. My green cord trousers came next, followed by my fawn Kickers boots, lables removed as from everything I wear because I refuse to be a walking advertisement for anybody. My combat jacket, knife, bags, catapult and other equipment I took down to the kitchen with me.

It was still early, and the rain I'd heard forecast the previous night was looking about ready to drop. I had my modest breakfast, and I was ready.

I went out into the fresh damp morning, walking quickly to keep warm and get round the island before any rain started. The hills beyond the town were hidden by cloud, and the sea was rough as the wind freshened. The grass was heavy with dew; drops of mist bowed the unopened flowers and clung to my Sacrifice Poles, too, like clear blood on the shrivelled heads and tiny, desiccated bodies.

A couple of jets screamed over the island at one point, two Jaguars wing to wing about one hundred metres up and going fast, crossing the whole island in an eye-blink and racing out to sea. I glared at them, then went on my way. Once they made me jump, another couple of them, a couple of years ago. They came in illegally low after bombing practice on the range just down the firth, blasting over the island so suddenly that I jumped while in the delicate manoeuvre of teasing a wasp into a jar from the old tree stump near the ruined sheep-pen at the north end of the island. The wasp stung me.

I went into town that day, bought an extra plastic model of a Jaguar, made the kit up that afternoon and ceremonially blew it to pieces on the roof of the Bunker with a small pipe-bomb. Two weeks later a Jaguar crashed into the sea off Nairn, though the pilot ejected in time. I'd like to think the Power was working then, but I suspect it was coincidence; high-performance jets crash so often it was no real surprise my symbolic and their real destruction came within a fortnight of each other.

I sat on the earth banking that looks out over the Muddy Creek and ate an apple. I leaned back on the young tree that as a sapling had been the Killer. It was grown now, and a good bit taller than me, but when I was young and we were the same size it had been my static catapult defending the southerly approaches to the island. Then, as now, it looked out over the broad creek and the gunmetal-coloured mud with the eaten-looking wreck of an old fishing boat sticking out of it.

After the Tale of Old Saul I put the catapult to another use, and it became the Killer; scourge of hamsters, mice and gerbils.

I remember that it could whack a fist-sized stone well over the creek and twenty metres or more into the undulating ground on the mainland, and once I got keyed into its natural rhythm I could send off a shot every two seconds. I could place them anywhere within a sixty-degree angle by varying the direction in which I pulled the sapling over and down. I didn't use a little animal every two seconds; they were expended at a few a week. For six months I was the best customer the Porteneil Pet Shop had, going in every Saturday to get a couple of beasts, and about every month buying a tube of badminton shuttlecocks from the toyshop as well. I doubt anybody ever put the two together, apart from me.

It was all for a purpose, of course; little that I do is not, one way or another. I was looking for Old Saul's skull.

I threw the core of the apple over the creek; it plopped into the mud on the far bank with a satisfying slurp. I decided it was time to look into the Bunker properly, and set off along the bank at a jog, swinging round the southernmost dune towards the old pillbox. I stopped to look at the shore. There didn't seem to be anything interesting there, but I remembered the lesson of the day before, when I had stopped to sniff the air and everything had seemed fine, then ten minutes later I was wrestling with a kamikaze rabbit, so I trotted down off the side of the dune and down to the line of debris thrown up by the sea.

There was one bottle. A very minor enemy, and empty. I went down to the water-line and threw the bottle out. It bobbed, head up, ten metres out. The tide hadn't covered the pebbles yet, so I took up a handful and lobbed them at the bottle. It was close enough to use the under-arm style, and the pebbles I'd selected were all of roughly the same size, so my fire was very accurate: four shots within splashing distance and a fifth which smashed the neck off the bottle. A small victory really, because the decisive defeat of the bottles had come about long ago, shortly after I learned to throw, when I first realised the sea was an enemy. It still tried me out now and again, though, and I was in no mood to allow even the slightest encroachment on my territory.

The bottle sunk, I returned to the dunes, went to the top of the one the Bunker lay half-buried in, and had a look round with my binoculars. The coast was clear, even if the weather wasn't. I went down to the Bunker.

I repaired the steel door years ago, loosening the rusted hinges and straightening the guides for the bolt. I took out the key to the padlock and opened the door. Inside there was the familiar waxy, burned smell. I closed the door and propped a piece of wood against it, then stood for a while, letting my eyes adjust to the gloom and my mind to the feel of the place.

After a while I could see dimly by the light filtering through the sacking hung over the two narrow slits which are the Bunker's only windows. I took off my shoulder bag and binoculars and hung them on nails hammered into the slightly crumbling concrete. I took up the tin with the matches in it and lit the candles; they burned yellowly and I knelt, clenching my fists and thinking. I'd found the candle-making kit in the cupboard under the stairs five or six years ago, and experimented with the colours and consistencies for months before hitting on the idea of using the wax as a wasp-prison. I looked up then and saw the head of a wasp poking up from the top of a candle on the altar. The newly lit candle, blood red and as thick as my wrist, contained the still flame and the tiny head within its caldera of wax like pieces of an alien game. As I watched, the flame, a centimetre behind the wasp's wax-gummed head, freed the antennae from the grease and they came upright for a while before they frazzled. The head started to smoke as the wax dribbled off it, then the fumes caught light, and the wasp body, a second flame within the crater, flickered and crackled as the fire incinerated the insect from its head down.

I lit the candle inside the skull of Old Saul. That orb of

47

bone, holed and yellowing, was what killed all those little creatures who met their death in the mud on the far side of the creek. I watched the smoky flame waver inside the place where the dog's brains used to be and I closed my eyes. I saw the Rabbit Grounds again, and the flaming bodies as they jumped and sped. I saw again the one that escaped the Grounds and died just before it made it to the stream. I saw the Black Destroyer, and remembered its demise. I thought of Eric, and wondered what the Factory's warning was about.

I saw myself, Frank L. Cauldhame, and I saw myself as I might have been: a tall slim man, strong and determined and making his way in the world, assured and purposeful. I opened my eyes and gulped, breathing deeply. A fetid light blazed from Old Saul's sockets. The candles on either side of the altar flickered with the skull-flame in a draught.

I looked round the Bunker. The severed heads of gulls, rabbits, crows, mice, owls, moles and small lizards looked down on me. They hung drying on short loops of black thread suspended from lengths of string stretched across the walls from corner to corner, and dim shadows turned slowly on the walls behind them. Around the foot of the walls, on plinths of wood or stone, or on bottles and cans the sea had surrendered, my collection of skulls watched me. The yellow brain-bones of horses, dogs, birds, fish and horned sheep faced in towards Old Saul, some with beaks and jaws open, some shut, the teeth exposed like drawn claws. To the right of the brick, wood and concrete altar where the candles and the skull sat were my small phials of precious fluids; to the left rose a tall set of clear plastic drawers designed to hold screws, washers, nails and hooks. Each drawer, not much larger than a small matchbox, held the body of a wasp which had been through the Factory.

I reached over for a large tin on my right, prised the tight lid off with my knife and used a small teaspoon inside to place some of the white mixture from the tin on to a round metal plate in front of the old dog's skull. Then I took the oldest of the wasp cadavers from its little tray and tipped it on to the white pile of granules. I replaced the sealed tin and the plastic drawer and lit the tiny pyre with a match.

The mixture of sugar and weedkiller sizzled and glared; the

intense light seared through me and clouds of smoke rolled up and around my head as I held my breath and my eyes watered. In a second the blaze was over, the mixture and the wasp a single black lump of scarred and blistered debris cooling from a bright yellow heat. I closed my eyes to inspect the patterns, but only the burning after-image remained, fading like the glow on the metal plate. It danced about briefly on my retinas, then disappeared. I had hoped for Eric's face, or some further clue about what was going to happen, but I got nothing.

I leaned forward, blew out the wasp candles, right then left, then blew through one eye and extinguished the candle inside the dog skull. Still glare-blind, I felt my way to the door through the dark and the smoke. I went out, letting the smoke and fumes free into the damp air; coils of blue and grey curled off my hair and clothes as I stood there, breathing deeply. I closed my eyes for a bit, then went back into the Bunker to tidy up.

I closed the door and locked it. I went back to the house for lunch and found my father chopping driftwood in the back garden.

'Good day,' he said, wiping his brow. It was humid if not particularly warm, and he was stripped to the vest.

'Hello,' I said.

'Were you all right yesterday?'

'I was.'

'I didn't get back till late.'

'I was asleep.'

'I thought you might be. You'll be wanting some lunch.'

'I'll make it today, if you want.'

'No, that's all right. You can chop the wood if you have a mind to. I'll make lunch for us.' He put the axe down and wiped his hands on his trousers, eyeing me. 'Was everything quiet yesterday?'

'Oh, yes,' I nodded, standing there.

'Nothing happened?'

'Nothing special,' I assured him, putting down my gear and taking my jacket off. I took up the axe. 'Very quiet, in fact.'

'Good,' he said, apparently convinced, and went into the

49

house. I started swinging the axe at the lumps of driftwood.

After lunch I went into town, taking Gravel my bike and some money. I told my father I'd be back before dinner. It started to rain when I was halfway to Porteneil, so I stopped to put on my ka-gool. The going was heavy but I got there without mishap. The town was grey and empty in the dull afternoon light; cars swished through on the road going north, some with their headlights on, making everything else seem even dimmer. I went to the gun and tackle shop first, to see old Mackenzie and take another of his American hunting-catapults off him, and some air-gun pellets, too.

'And how are you today, young man?'

'Very well, and yourself?'

'Och, not too bad, you know,' he said, shaking his grey head slowly, his yellowed eyes and hair rather sickly in the electric light of the shop. We always say the same things to each other. Often I stay longer in the shop than I mean to because it smells so good.

'And how's that uncle of yours these days? I haven't seen him for – oh, a while.'

'He's well.'

'Oh, good, good,' Mr Mackenzie said, screwing up his eyes with a slightly pained expression and nodding slowly. I nodded, too, and looked at my watch.

'Well, I must be going,' I said, and started to back off, putting my new catapult into the day-pack on my back and stuffing the pellets wrapped in brown paper into my combat-jacket pockets.

'Oh, well, if you must, you must,' said Mackenzie, nodding at the glass counter as though inspecting the flies, reels and duck-calls within. He took up a cloth by the side of the cash register and started to move it slowly over the surface, looking up just once as I left the shop, saying, 'Goodbye, then.'

'Yes, goodbye.'

In the Firthview café, apparently the location of some awful and localised ground subsidence since it was named, because it would have to be at least a storey taller to catch a view of the

50

water, I had a cup of coffee and a game of Space Invaders. They had a new machine in, but after a pound or so I had mastered it and won an extra spaceship. I got bored with it and sat down with my coffee.

I inspected the posters on the café walls to see if there was anything interesting happening in the area in the near future, but apart from the Film Club there wasn't much. The next showing was *The Tin Drum,* but that was a book my father had bought for me years ago, one of the few real presents he has ever given me, and I had therefore assiduously avoided reading it, just as I had *Myra Breckinridge,* another of his rare gifts. Mostly my father just gives me the money that I ask for and lets me get what I want for myself. I don't think he's really interested; but, on the other hand, he wouldn't refuse me anything. As far as I can tell, we have some sort of unspoken agreement that I keep quiet about not officially existing in return for being able to do more or less as I like on the island and buy more or less what I like in the town. The only thing we had argued about recently was the motorbike, which he said he would buy me when I was a bit older. I suggested that it might be a good idea to get it in midsummer so that I could get plenty of practice in before the skiddy weather set in, but he thought there might be too much tourist traffic going through the town and on the roads around it in the middle of the summer. I think he just wants to keep putting it off; he might be frightened of me gaining too much independence, or he might simply be scared that I'll kill myself the way a lot of youths seem to when they get a bike. I don't know; I never know exactly how much he really feels for me. Come to think of it, I never know exactly how much I really feel for him.

I had rather been hoping that I might see somebody I knew while I was in the town, but the only people I saw were old Mackenzie in the gun and tackle shop and Mrs Stuart in the café, yawning and fat behind her Formica counters and reading a Mills & Boon. Not that I know all that many people anyway, I suppose; Jamie is my only real friend, though through him I have met a few people of about my own age I regard as acquaintances. Not going to school, and having to pretend I didn't live on the island all the time, has meant that I

51

didn't grow up with anybody of my own age (except Eric, of course, but even he was away for a long time), and about the time I was thinking of venturing further afield and getting to know more people Eric went crazy, and things got a bit uncomfortable in the town for a while.

Mothers told their children to behave or *Eric Cauldhame* would get them and do horrible things to them with worms and maggots. As I suppose was inevitable, the story gradually became that Eric would set fire to them, not just their pet dogs; and, as was probably also inevitable, a lot of kids started to think that *I* was Eric, or that I got up to the same tricks. Or perhaps their parents guessed about Blyth, Paul and Esmerelda. Whatever, they would run from me, or shout rude things from a distance, so I kept a low profile and restricted my brief visits to the town to a taciturn minimum. I get the odd funny look to this day, from children, youths and adults, and I know some mothers tell their children to behave or '*Frank'll get you*,' but it doesn't bother me. I can take it.

I got on my bike and went back to the house a bit recklessly, shooting through puddles on the path and taking the Jump – a bit on the path where there's a long downhill on a dune and then a short uphill where it's easy to leave the ground – at a good forty kilometres per hour, landing with a muddy thump that nearly had me in the whin bushes and left me with a very sore bum, making me want to keep opening my mouth with the feeling of it. But I got back safely. I told my father I was all right and I'd be in for my dinner in an hour or so, then went back to the shed to wipe Gravel down. After I'd done that I made up some new bombs to replace the ones I'd used the day before, and a few extra besides. I put the old electric fire on in the shed, not so much to warm me as to keep the highly hygroscopic mixture from absorbing moisture out of a damp air.

What I'd really like, of course, is not to have to bother with lugging kilo bags of sugar and tins of weedkiller back from the town to stuff into electrical-conduit piping which Jamie the dwarf gets for me from the building contractor's where he works in Porteneil. With a cellar full of enough cordite to wipe half the island off the map it does seem a bit daft, but my father won't let me near the stuff.

It was his father, Colin Cauldhame, who got the cordite from the ship-breaking yard there used to be down the coast. One of his relations worked there, and had found some old warship with one magazine still loaded with the explosive. Colin bought the cordite and used it to light fires with. Uncontained, cordite makes a very good firelighter. Colin bought enough to last the house about two hundred years, even if his son had continued using it, so perhaps he was thinking of selling it. I know that my father did use it for a while, lighting the stove with it, but he hasn't for a while. God knows how much there still is down there; I've seen great stacks and bales of it still with the Royal Navy markings on it, and I've dreamed up any number of ways of getting at it, but short of tunnelling in from the shed and taking the cordite out from the back, so that the bales looked untouched from the inside of the cellar, I don't see how I could do it. My father checks the cellar every few weeks, going nervously down with a torch, counting the bales and sniffing, and looking at the thermometer and hygrometer.

It's nice and cool inside the cellar, and not damp, though I guess it can only be just above the water table, and my father seems to know what he's doing and is confident that the explosive hasn't become unstable, but I think he's nervous about it and has been ever since the Bomb Circle. (Guilty again; that was my fault, too. My second murder, the one when I think some of the family started to suspect.) If he's that frightened, though, I don't know why he doesn't just throw it out. But I think he's got his own little superstition about the cordite. Something about a link with the past, or an evil demon we have lurking, a symbol for all our family misdeeds; waiting, perhaps, one day, to surprise us.

Anyway, I have no access to it, and have to cart metres of black metal piping back from the town and sweat and labour over it, bending it and cutting it and boring it and crimping it and bending it again, straining with it in the vice until the bench and shed creak with my efforts. I suppose it's a craft in some ways, and certainly it is quite skilled, but I get bored with it sometimes, and only thinking of the use I'll put those little black torpedoes to keeps me heaving and bending away.

I tidied everything away and cleaned the shed up after my bomb-making activity, then went in for dinner.

'They're searching for him,' my father said suddenly, in between mouthfuls of cabbage and soya chunks. His dark eyes flickered at me like a long sooty flame, then he looked down again. I drank some of the beer I had opened. The new batch of home-brew tasted better than the last lot, and stronger.

'Eric?'

'Yes, Eric. They're looking for him on the moors.'

'On the moors?'

'They think he might be on the moors.'

'Yes, that would account for them looking for him there.'

'Indeed,' my father nodded. 'Why are you humming?'

I cleared my throat and kept on eating my burgers, pretending I hadn't heard him properly.

'I was thinking,' he said, then spooned some more of the green-brown mixture into his face and chewed for a long time. I waited to hear what he was going to say next. He waved his spoon slackly, pointing it vaguely upstairs, then said: 'How long would you say the flex on the telephone is?'

'Loose or stretched?' I said quickly, putting down my glass of beer. He grunted and said nothing else, going back to his plate of food, apparently satisfied if not pleased. I drank.

'Is there anything special you'd like me to order from the town?' he said eventually, as he rinsed his mouth with real orange juice. I shook my head, drank my beer.

'No, just the usual,' I shrugged.

'Instant potatoes and beefburgers and sugar and mince pies and cornflakes and junk like that, I suppose.' My father sneered slightly, though it was said evenly enough.

I nodded. 'Yes, that'll do fine. You know my likes.'

'You don't eat properly. I should have been more strict with you.'

I didn't say anything, but kept on eating slowly. I could tell that my father was looking at me from the other end of the table, swilling his juice round in his glass and staring at my head as I bent over my plate. He shook his head and got up from the table, taking his plate to the sink to rinse it.

'Are you going out tonight?' he asked, turning on the tap.

'No. I'll stay in tonight. Go out tomorrow night.'

'I hope you won't be getting steaming drunk again. You'll be arrested some night and then where will we be?' He looked at me. 'Eh?'

'I don't go getting steaming drunk,' I assured him. 'I just have a drink or two to be sociable and that's all.'

'Well, you're very noisy when you come back for somebody who's only been sociable, so you are.' He looked at me darkly again and sat down.

I shrugged. Of course I get drunk. What the hell's the point of drinking if you don't get drunk? But I'm careful; I don't want to cause any complications.

'Well, just you be careful, then. I always know how much you've had from your farts.' He snorted, as though imitating one.

My father has a theory about the link between mind and bowel being both crucial and very direct. It's another of his ideas which he keeps trying to interest people in; he has a manuscript on the subject ('The State of the Fart') which he also sends away to London to publishers now and again and which they of course send back by return. He has variously claimed that from farts he can tell not only what people have eaten or drunk, but also the sort of person they are, what they *ought* to eat, whether they are emotionally unstable or upset, whether they are keeping secrets, laughing at you behind your back or trying to ingratiate themselves with you, and even what they are thinking about at the precise moment they issue the fart (this largely from the sound). All total nonsense.

'H'm,' I said, non-committal to a fault.

'Oh, I can,' he said as I finished my meal and leaned back, wiping my mouth on the back of my hand, more to annoy him that anything else. He kept nodding. 'I know when you've had Heavy, or Lager. And I've smelt Guinness off you, too.'

'I don't drink Guinness,' I lied, secretly impressed. 'I'm afraid of getting athlete's throat.'

This witticism was lost on him apparently, for without a pause he continued: 'It's just money down the drain, you know. Don't expect me to finance your alcoholism.'

'Oh, you're being silly,' I said, and stood up.

'I know what I'm talking about. I've seen better men than you think they could handle the drink and end up in the gutter with a bottle of the fortified wine.'

If that last sally was intended to go below the belt, it failed; the 'better men than you' line was worked out long ago.

'Well, it's my life, isn't it?' I said and, putting my plate in the sink, left the kitchen. My father said nothing.

That night I watched television and did some paperwork, amending the maps to include the newly named Black Destroyer Hill, writing a brief description of what I'd done to the rabbits and logging both the effects of the bombs that I'd used and the manufacture of the latest batch. I determined to keep the Polaroid with the War Bag in future; for low-risk punitive expeditions like that against the rabbits it would more than repay the extra weight and the amount of time consumed using it. Of course, for serious devilry the War Bag has to go by itself, and a camera would just be a liability, but I haven't had a real threat for a couple of years, since the time some big boys in the town took to bullying me in Porteneil and ambushing me on the path.

I thought things were going to get pretty heavy for a while, but they never did escalate the way I thought they might. I threatened them with my knife once, after they stopped me on my bike and started pushing me around and demanding money. They backed off that time, but a few days later they tried to invade the island. I held them off with steelies and stones, and they fired back with air-guns, and for a while it was quite exciting, but then Mrs Clamp came with the weekly messages and threatened to call the police, and after calling her a few nasty names they left.

I started the cache system then, building up supplies of steelies, stones, bolts and lead fishing-weights buried in plastic bags and boxes at strategic points around the island. I also set up snares and trip-wires linked to glass bottles in the grass on the dunes over the creek, so that if anybody tried to sneak up they would either catch themselves or snag the wire, pulling the bottle out of its hole in the sand and down on to a stone. I sat up for the next few nights, my head poking out of the back skylight of the loft, my ears straining for the tinkle of glass breaking or muffled curses, or the more usual signal of the birds being disturbed and taking flight, but nothing more happened. I just avoided the boys in the town for a while, only going in with my father or at times when I knew they would be in school.

The cache system survives, and I've even added a couple of petrol bombs to one or two of the secret stores, where a likely avenue of attack comes in over terrain the bottles would smash on, but the trip-wires I've dismantled and left in the shed. My Defence Manual, which contains things like maps of the island with the caches marked, likely attack routes, a summary of tactics, a list of weapons I have or might make, includes within this last category quite a few unpleasant things like trip-wires and snares set a body-length away from a concealed broken bottle sticking up in the grass, electrically detonated mines made from pipe-bombs and small nails, all buried in the sand, and a few interesting, if unlikely, secret weapons, like frisbees with razors embedded in the edge.

Not that I want to kill anybody now, but it is all for defence rather than offence, and it does make me feel a lot more secure. Soon I'll have enough money for a really powerful crossbow, and that I'm certainly looking forward to; it'll help make up for the fact that I've never been able to persuade my father to buy a rifle or a shotgun that I could use sometimes. I have my catapults and slings and air-rifle, and they could all be lethal in the right circumstances, but they just don't have the long-range hitting power I really hanker after. The pipe-bombs are the same. They have to be placed, or at best thrown at the target, and even slinging some of the purpose-built smaller ones is inaccurate and slow. I can imagine some unpleasant things happening with the sling, too; the sling-bombs have to be on a pretty short fuse if they're to detonate soon enough after they land not to be throw-backable, and I've had a couple of close calls already when they've gone off just after they left the sling.

I've experimented with guns, of course, both mere

projectile weapons and mortars which would lob the sling-bombs, but they have all been clumsy, dangerous, slow and rather prone to blowing up.

A shotgun would be ideal, though I'd settle for a .22 rifle, but a crossbow will just have to do. Perhaps sometime I'll be able to devise a way round my official non-existence and apply for a gun myself, though even then, all things considered, I might not be granted a licence. Oh, to be in America, I occasionally think.

I was logging the cache petrol bombs which hadn't been inspected for evaporation recently when the phone went. I looked at my watch, surprised at the lateness of the hour: nearly eleven. I ran downstairs to the phone, hearing my father coming to the door of his room as I passed it.

'Porteneil 531.' Pips sounded.

'Fuck it, Frank, I've got luna maria callouses on me feet. How the hell are ye, me young bucko?'

I looked at the handset, then up at my father, who was leaning over the rail from the floor above, tucking his pyjama top into his trousers. I spoke into the phone: 'Hello there, Jamie, what are you doing calling me this late?'

'Wha—? Oh, the old man's there, is he?' Eric said. 'Tell him he's a bag of effervescent pus, from me.'

'Jamie sends his regards,' I called up to my father, who turned without a word and went back to his room. I heard the door close. I turned back to the phone. 'Eric, where are you this time?'

'Ah, shit, I'm not telling you. Guess.'

'Well, *I* don't know. . . . Glasgow?'

'Ah ha ha ha ha ha!' Eric cackled. I clenched plastic.

'How are you? Are you all right?'

'I'm fine. How are you?'

'Great. Look, how are you eating? Have you got any money? Are you hitching lifts or what? They're looking for you, you know, but there hasn't been anything on the news yet. You haven't—' I stopped before I said something he might take exception to.

'I'm doing fine. I eat dogs! Heh heh heh!'

I groaned. 'Oh, God, you're not really, are you?'

'What else can I eat? It's great, Frankie boy; I'm keeping to the fields and the woods and walking a lot and getting lifts and when I get near a town I look for a good fat juicy dog and I make friends with it and take it out to the woods and then I kill it and eat it. What could be simpler? I do love the outdoor life.'

'You are *cooking* them, aren't you?'

'Of course I'm fucking cooking them,' Eric said indignantly. 'What do you think I am?'

'Is that all you're eating?'

'No. I steal things. Shoplift. It's so easy. I steal things I can't eat, just for the hell of it. Like tampons and plastic dustbin-liners and party-size packets of crisps and one hundred cocktail sticks and twelve cake-candles in various colours and photograph frames and steering-wheel covers in simulated leather and towel-holders and fabric-softeners and double-action air-fresheners to waft away those lingering kitchen smells and cute little boxes for awkward odds and ends and packs of cassettes and lockable petrol-caps and record-cleaners and telephone indexes slimming magazines pot-holders packs of name-labels artificial eyelashes make-up boxes anti-smoking mixture toy watches—'

'Don't you like crisps?' I broke in quickly.

'Eh?' He sounded confused.

'You mentioned party-size packets of crisps as being something you couldn't eat.'

'For Christ's sake, Frank, could *you* eat a party-size packet of crisps?'

'And how are you keeping?' I said quickly. 'I mean, you must be sleeping rough. Aren't you catching cold or something?'

'I'm not sleeping.'

'You're not *sleeping*?'

'Of course not. You don't have to sleep. That's just something *they* tell you to keep *control* over you. Nobody has to sleep; you're *taught* to sleep when you're a kid. If you're really determined, you can get over it. I've got over the need to sleep. I never sleep now. That way it's a lot easier to keep watch and make sure they don't *creep up* on you, and you can keep going as well. Nothing like keeping going. You become like a ship.'

'Like a ship?' Now I was confused.

'Stop repeating everything I say, Frank.' I heard him put more money into the box. 'I'll teach you how not to sleep when I get back.'

'Thanks. When do you expect to get here?'

'Sooner or later. Ha ha ha ha ha!'

'Look, Eric, why are you eating dogs if you can steal all that stuff?'

'I've already told you, you *idiot*; you can't eat any of that crap.'

'But, then, why not steal stuff you can eat and don't steal the stuff you can't and don't bother with the dogs?' I suggested. I already knew it wasn't a good idea; I could hear the tone of my voice rising higher and higher as I spoke the sentence, and that was always a sign I was getting into some sort of verbal mess.

Eric shouted: 'Are you *crazy*? What's the matter with you? What's the point of that? These are *dogs*, aren't they? It isn't as though I was killing cats or fieldmice or goldfish or anything. I'm talking about *dogs*, you rabid dingbat! *Dogs!*'

'You don't have to shout at me,' I said evenly, though starting to get angry myself. 'I was only asking why you waste so much time stealing stuff you can't eat and then waste more time stealing dogs when you could steal and eat at the same time, as it were.'

' "As it were"? *"As it were"*? What the hell are you gibbering about?' Eric yelled, his strangled voice hoarse and contralto.

'Oh, don't start screaming,' I moaned, putting my other hand over my forehead and through my hair, closing my eyes.

'I'll scream if I want to!' Eric screamed. 'What do you think I'm doing all this for? Eh? What the hell do you think I'm doing all this for? These are *dogs*, you brainless little shitbag! Haven't you any brains left? What's happened to all your *brains*, Frankie boy? Cat got your tongue? I said, Cat got your *tongue*?'

'Don't start banging the—' I said, not really into the mouthpiece.

'Eeeeeeaaarrrggghhh Bllleeeaarrrgggrrllleeeooouurrgghh!' Eric spat and choked down the line, and there followed the noise of the phone-box handset being smashed around the inside of the booth. I sighed and replaced the receiver thoughtfully. I just didn't seem to be able to handle Eric on the telephone.

I went back to my room, trying to forget about my brother; I wanted to get to bed early so that I could be up in time for the naming ceremony of the new catapult. I'd think about a better way to handle Eric once I had that out of the way.

. . . Like a ship, indeed. What a loony.

4: The Bomb Circle

OFTEN I've thought of myself as a state; a country or, at the very least, a city. It used to seem to me that the different ways I felt sometimes about ideas, courses of action and so on were like the differing political moods that countries go through. It has always seemed to me that people vote in a new government not because they actually agree with their politics but just because they want a change. Somehow they think that things will be better under the new lot. Well, people are stupid, but it all seems to have more to do with mood, caprice and atmosphere than carefully thought-out arguments. I can feel the same sort of thing going on in my head. Sometimes the thoughts and feelings I had didn't really agree with each other, so I decided I must be lots of different people inside my brain.

For example, there has always been a part of me which has felt guilty about killing Blyth, Paul and Esmerelda. That same part feels guilty now about taking revenge on innocent rabbits because of one rogue male. But I liken it to an opposition party in a parliament, or a critical press; acting as a conscience and a brake, but not in power and unlikely to assume it. Another part of me is racist, probably because I've hardly met any colored people and all I know of them is what I read in papers and see on television, where black people are usually talked of in terms of numbers and presumed guilty until proved innocent. This part of me is still quite strong, though of course I know there is no logical reason for race hatred. Whenever I see coloured people in Porteneil, buying souvenirs or stopping off for a snack, I hope that they will ask me something so that I can show how polite I am and prove that my reasoning is stronger than my more crass instincts, or training.

By the same token, though, there was no *need* to take revenge on the rabbits. There never is, even in the big world. I think reprisals against people only distantly or circumstant-ially connected with those who have done others wrong are to make the people doing the avenging feel good. Like the death penalty, you want it because it makes *you* feel better, not because it's a deterrent or any nonsense like that.

At least the rabbits won't know that Frank Cauldhame did what he did to them, the way a community of people knows what the baddies did to them, so that the revenge ends up having the opposite effect from that intended, inciting rather than squashing resistance. At least I admit that it's all to boost my ego, restore my pride and give me pleasure, not to save the country or uphold justice or honour the dead.

So there were parts of me that watched the naming ceremony for the new catapult with some amusement, even contempt. In that state inside my head, this is like intellectuals in a country sneering at religion while not being able to deny the effect it has on the mass of people. In the ceremony I smeared the metal, rubber and plastic of the new device with earwax, snot, blood, urine, belly-button fluff and toenail cheese, christened it by firing the empty sling at a wingless wasp crawling on the face of the Factory, and also fired it at my bared foot, raising a bruise.

Parts of me thought all this was nonsense, but they were in a tiny minority. The rest of me knew this sort of thing *worked*. It gave me power, it made me part of what I own and where I am. It makes me feel good.

I found a photograph of Paul as a baby in one of the albums I kept in the loft, and after the ceremony I wrote the name of the new catapult on the back of the picture, scrunched it up around a steelie and secured it with a little tape, then went down, out of the loft and the house, into the chill drizzle of a new day.

I went to the cracked end of the old slipway at the north end of the island. I pulled the rubber almost to maximum and sent the ball-bearing and photograph hissing and spinning way out to sea. I didn't see the splash.

The catapult ought to be safe so long as nobody knew its name. That didn't help the Black Destroyer, certainly, but it died because I made a mistake, and my power is so strong that when it goes wrong, which is seldom but not never, even those things I have invested with great protective power become vulnerable. Again, in that head-state, I could feel anger that I could have made such a mistake, and a determination it wouldn't happen again. This was like a general who had lost a battle or some important territory being disciplined or shot.

Well, I had done what I could to protect the new catapult and, while I was sorry that what had happened at the Rabbit Grounds had cost me a trusted weapon with many battle honours to its name (not to mention a significant sum out of the Defence budget), I thought that maybe what had happened had been for the best. The part of me which made the mistake with the buck, letting it get the better of me for a moment, might still be around if that acid test hadn't found it out. The incompetent or misguided general had been dismissed. Eric's return might call for all my reactions and powers to be at their peak of efficiency.

It was still very early and, although the mist and drizzle should have had me feeling a little mellow, I was still in good and confident spirits from the naming ceremony.

I felt like a Run, so I left my jacket near the Pole I'd been at the day Diggs had come with the news, and tucked the catapult tightly between my cords and my belt. I tugged my boots to running tension after checking my socks were straight and unruffled, then jogged slowly down to the line of hard sand between the seaweed tidelines. The drizzle was coming and going and the sun was visible occasionally through the mist and cloud as a red and hazy disc. There was a slight wind coming from the north, and I turned into it. I powered up gradually, settling into an easy, long-paced stride that got my lungs working properly and readied my legs. My arms, fists clenched, moved with a fluid rhythm, sending first one then the other shoulder forward. I breathed deeply, padding over the sand. I came to the braided reaches of the river where it swung out over the sands, and adjusted my steps so that I cleared all the channels easily and cleanly, a leap at a time. Once over, I put my head down and increased speed. My head and fists rammed the air, my feet flexed, flung, gripped and pushed.

The air whipped at me, little gusts of drizzle stinging slightly as I hit them. My lungs exploded, imploded, exploded, imploded; plumes of wet sand flew from my soles, rising as I sped on, falling in little curves and spattering back as I raced on into the distance. I brought my face up and put my head back, baring my neck to the wind like a lover, to the rain like an offering. My breath rasped in my throat, and a slight light-headedness I had started to feel owing to hyperoxygenating earlier waned as my muscles took up the slack of the extra power in my blood. I boosted, increasing speed as the jagged line of dead seaweed and old wood and cans and bottles skittered by me; I felt like a bead on a thread being pulled through the air on a line, sucked along by throat and lungs and legs, a continual pounce of flowing energy. I kept the boost up as long as I could; then, when I felt it start to go, relaxed, and went back to merely running fast for a while.

I charged across the sands, the dunes to my left moving by like stands on a racetrack. Ahead I could see the Bomb Circle, where I would stop or turn. I boosted again, head down and shouting to myself inside, screaming mentally, my voice like a press, screwing down tighter to squeeze a final effort from my legs. I *flew* across the sands, body tilted crazily forward, lungs bursting, legs pounding.

The moment passed and I slowed quickly, dropping to a trot as I approached the Bomb Circle, almost staggering into it, then flinging myself on to the sand inside to lie panting, heaving, gasping, staring at the grey sky and invisible drizzle, spreadeagled in the centre of the rocks. My chest rose and fell, my heart pounded inside its cage. A dull roaring filled my ears, and my whole body tingled and buzzed. My leg muscles seemed to be in some daze of quivering tension. I let my head fall to one side, my cheek against the cool damp sand.

I wondered what it felt like to die.

The Bomb Circle, my dad's leg and his stick, his reluctance to get me a motorbike perhaps, the candles in the skull, the legions of dead mice and hamsters – they're all the fault of Agnes, my father's second wife and my mother.

I can't remember my mother, because if I did I'd hate her. As it is, I hate her name, the idea of her. It was she who let the Stoves take Eric away to Belfast, away from the island, away from what he knew. They thought that my father was a bad parent because he dressed Eric in girl's clothes and let him run wild, and my mother let them take him because she didn't like children in general and Eric in particular; she thought he was bad for her karma in some way. Probably the same dislike of children led her to desert me immediately after my birth, and also caused her only to return on that one, fateful occasion when she was at least partly responsible for my little accident. All in all, I think I have good reason to hate her. I lay there in the Bomb Circle where I killed her other son, and I hoped that she was dead, too.

I went back at a slow run, glowing with energy and feeling even better than I had at the start of the Run. I was already looking forward to going out in the evening – a few drinks and a chat to Jamie, my friend, and some sweaty, ear-ringing music at the Arms. I did one short sprint, just to shake my head as I ran and get some of the sand out of my hair, then relaxed to a trot once more.

The rocks of the Bomb Circle usually get me thinking and this time was no exception, especially considering the way I'd lain down inside them like some Christ or something, opened to the sky, dreaming of death. Well, Paul went about as quickly as you can go; I was certainly humane that time. Blyth had lots of time to realise what was happening, jumping about the Snake Park screaming as the frantic and enraged snake bit his stump repeatedly, and little Esmerelda must have had some inkling what was going to happen to her as she was slowly blown away.

My brother Paul was five when I killed him. I was eight. It was over two years after I had subtracted Blyth with an adder that I found an opportunity to get rid of Paul. Not that I bore him any personal ill-will; it was simply that I knew he couldn't stay. I knew I'd never be free of the dog until he was gone (Eric, poor well-meaning bright but ignorant Eric, thought I still wasn't, and I just couldn't tell him why I knew I was).

Paul and I had gone for a walk along the sand, northwards on a calm, bright autumn day after a ferocious storm the night before that had ripped slates off the roof of the house, torn up one of the trees by the old sheep-pen and even snapped one of the cables on the suspension foot-bridge. Father got Eric to help him with the clearing-up and repairs while I took myself and Paul out from under their feet.

I always got on well with Paul. Perhaps because I knew from an early age that he was not long for this world, I tried to make his time in it as pleasant as possible, and thus ended up treating him far better than most young boys treat their younger brothers.

We saw that the storm had changed a lot of things as soon as we came to the river that marks the end of the island; it had swollen hugely, carving immense channels out of the sand, great surging brown trenches of water streaming by and tearing lumps from the banks continually and sweeping them away. We had to walk right down almost to the sea at its low-tide limit before we could get across. We went on, me holding Paul by the hand, no malice in my heart. Paul was singing to himself and asking questions of the type children tend to, such as why weren't the birds all blown away during the storm, and why didn't the sea fill up with water with the stream going so hard?

As we walked along the sand in the quietness, stopping to

look at all the interesting things which had been washed up, the beach gradually disappeared. Where the sand had stretched in an unbroken line of gold towards the horizon, now we saw more and more rock exposed the farther up the strand we looked, until in the distance the dunes faced a shore of pure stone. The storm had swept all the sand away during the night, starting just past the river and continuing farther than the places I had names for or had ever seen. It was an impressive sight, and one that frightened me a little at first, just because it was such a huge change and I was worried that it might happen to the island sometime. I remembered, however, that my father had told me of this sort of thing happening in the past, and the sands had always returned over the following few weeks and months.

Paul had great fun running and jumping from rock to rock and throwing stones into pools between the rocks. Rock pools were something of a novelty for him. We went farther up the wasted beach, still finding interesting pieces of flotsam and finally coming to the rusted remnant I thought was a water-tank or a half-buried canoe, from a distance. It stuck out of a patch of sand, jutting at a steep angle, about a metre and a half of it exposed. Paul was trying to catch fish in a pool as I looked at the thing.

I touched the side of the tapered cylinder wonderingly, feeling something very calm and strong about it, though I didn't know why. Then I stepped back and looked again at it. Its shape became clear, and I could then guess roughly how much of it must still be buried under the sand. It was a bomb, stood on its tail.

I went back to it carefully, stroking it gently and making shushing noises with my mouth. It was rust-red and black with its rotund decay, smelling dank and casting a shell-shadow. I followed the line of the shadow along the sand, over the rocks, and found myself looking at little Paul, splashing happily about in a pool, slapping the water with a great flat bit of wood almost as big as he was. I smiled, called him over.

'See this?' I said. It was a rhetorical question. Paul nodded, big eyes staring. 'This', I told him, 'is a bell. Like the ones in the church in the town. The noise we hear on a Sunday, you know?'

'Yes. Just after brekast, Frank?'

'What?'

'The noise jus affer *Sum*day *brek*ast, Frank.' Paul hit me lightly on the knee with a podgy hand.

I nodded. 'Yes, that's right. Bells make that noise. They're great big hollow bits of metal filled up with noises and they let the noises out on Sunday mornings after breakfast. That's what this is.'

'A brekast?' Paul looked up at me with mightily furrowed little brows. I shook my head patiently.

'No. A bell.'

'"B is for Bell," ' Paul said quietly, nodding to himself and staring at the rusting device. Probably remembering an old nursery-book. He was a bright child; my father intended to send him off to school properly when the time came, and had already started him learning the alphabet.

'That's right. Well, this old bell must have fallen off a ship, or perhaps it got washed out here in a flood. I know what we'll do; I'll go up on the dunes and you hit the bell with your bit of wood and we'll see if I can hear it. Will we do that? Would you like that? It'll be very loud and you might get frightened.'

I stooped down to put my face level with his. He shook his head violently and stuck his nose against mine. 'No! Won't get frigh' end!' he shouted. 'I'll—'

He was about to skip past me and hit the bomb with the piece of wood — he had already raised it above his head and made the lunge – when I reached out and caught him round the waist.

'Not *yet,*' I said. 'Wait until I'm farther away. It's an old bell and it might only have one good noise left in it. You don't want to waste it, do you?'

Paul wriggled, and the look on his face seemed to indicate that he wouldn't actually mind wasting anything, just so long as he got to hit the bell with his plank of wood. 'Aw-right,' he said, and stopped struggling. I put him down. 'But can I hit it really *really* hard?'

'As hard as you possibly can, when I wave from the top of the dune over there. All right?'

69

'Can I prakiss?'

'Practise by hitting the sand.'

'Can I hit the puddles?'

'Yes, practise hitting the pools of water. That's a good idea.'

'Can I hit *this* puddle?' He pointed with the wood at the circular sand-pool around the bomb. I shook my head.

'No, that might make the bell angry.'

He frowned. 'Do bells *get* an'ry?'

'Yes, they do. I'm going now. You hit the bell really hard and I'll listen really hard, right?'

'Yes, Frank.'

'You won't hit the bell until I wave, will you?'

He shook his head. 'Pomiss.'

'Good. Won't be long.' I turned and started to head for the dunes at a slow run. My back felt funny. I looked round as I went, checking there was nobody about. There were only a few gulls, though, wheeling in a sky shot with ragged clouds. Over my shoulder when I looked back, I saw Paul. He was still by the bomb, whacking the sand with his plank, using both hands to hold it and bringing it down with all his strength, jumping up in the air at the same time and yelling. I ran faster, over the rocks on to the firm sand, over the driftline and on up to the golden sand, slower and dry, then up to the grass on the nearest dune. I scrambled to the top and looked out over the sand and rocks to where Paul stood, a tiny figure against the reflected brightness of the pools and wet sands, overshadowed by the tilted cone of metal beside him. I stood up, waited until he noticed me, took one last look round, then waved my hands high over my head and threw myself flat.

While I was lying there, waiting, I realised that I hadn't told Paul *where* to hit the bomb. Nothing happened. I lay there feeling my stomach sinking slowly into the sand on the top of the dune. I sighed to myself and looked up.

Paul was a distant puppet, jerking and leaping and throwing back his arms and whacking the bomb repeatedly on the side. I could just hear his lusty yells over the whisper of the grass in the wind. 'Shit,' I said to myself, and put my hand under my chin just as Paul, after a quick glance in my direction, started to attack the nose of the bomb. He had hit it once and I had taken my hand

70

out from under my chin preparatory to ducking when Paul, the bomb and its little halo-pool and everything else for about ten metres around suddenly vanished inside a climbing column of sand and steam and flying rock, lit just the once from inside, in that blindingly brief first moment, by the high explosive detonating.

The rising tower of debris blossomed and drifted, starting to fall as the shockwave pulsed at me from the dune. I was vaguely aware of a lot of small sandslips along the drying faces of the nearby dunes. The noise rolled over then, a twisting crack and belly-rumble of thunder. I watched a gradually widening circle of splashes go out from the centre of the explosion as the debris came back to earth. The pillar of gas and sand was pulled out by the wind, darkening the sand under its shadow and forming a curtain of haze under its base like you see under a heavy cloud sometimes as it starts to get rid of its rain. I could see the crater now.

I ran down. I stood about fifty metres away from the still steaming crater. I didn't look too closely at any of the bits and pieces lying around, squinting at them from the side of my eye, wanting and not wanting to see bloody meat or tattered clothing. The noise rumbled back uncertainly from the hills beyond the town. The edge of the crater was marked with huge splinters of stone torn up from the bedrock under the sands; they stood like broken teeth around the scene, pointing at the sky or fallen slanted over. I watched the distant cloud from the explosion drift away over the firth, dispersing, then I turned and ran as fast as I could for the house.

So nowadays I can say it was a German bomb of five hundred kilograms and it was dropped by a crippled He. 111 trying to get back to its Norwegian base after an unsuccessful attack on the flying-boat base farther down the firth. I like to think it was the gun in my bunker that hit it and forced the pilot to turn tail and dump his bombs.

The tips of some of those great splinters of igneous rock still stick above the surface of the long-returned sand, and they form the Bomb Circle, poor dead Paul's most fitting monument: a blasphemous stone circle where the shadows play.

71

I was lucky, again. Nobody saw anything, and nobody could believe that I had *done* it. I was distracted with grief this time, torn by guilt, and Eric had to look after me while I acted my part to perfection, though I say it myself. I didn't enjoy deceiving Eric, but I knew it was necessary; I couldn't tell him I'd done it because he wouldn't have understood *why* I'd done it. He would have been horrified, and very likely never have been my friend again. So I had to act the tortured, self-blaming child, and Eric had to comfort me while my father brooded.

Actually, I didn't like the way Diggs questioned me about what had happened, and for a few moments I thought he might have guessed, but my replies seemed to satisfy him. It didn't help that I had to call my father 'uncle' and Eric and Paul 'cousins'; this was my father's idea of trying to fool the policeman about my parentage in case Diggs did any asking around and discovered that I didn't exist officially. My story was that I was the orphaned son of my father's long-lost younger brother, and only staying on occasional extended holidays on the island while I was passed from relative to relative and my future was decided.

Anyway, I got through this tricky interval, and even the sea co-operated for once, coming in just after the explosion and sweeping away any tell-tale tracks I might have left an hour or more before Diggs arrived from the village to inspect the scene.

Mrs Clamp was at the house when I got back, unloading the huge wicker hopper on the front of her ancient bike which lay propped against the kitchen table. She was busy stuffing our cupboards, the fridge and the freezer with the food and supplies she had brought from the town.

'Good morning, Mrs Clamp,' I said pleasantly as I entered the kitchen. She turned to look at me. Mrs Clamp is very old and extremely small. She looked me up and down and said, 'Oh, it's *you,* is it?' and turned back to the wicker hopper on the bike, delving into its depths with both hands, surfacing with long packages wrapped in newspaper. She staggered over to the freezer, climbed on to a small stool by its side, unwrapped the packages to reveal frozen packs of my beefburgers, and placed them in the freezer, leaning over it until she was almost inside. It struck me how easy it would be to — I shook my head clear of the silly thought. I sat down at the kitchen table to watch Mrs Clamp work.

'How are you keeping these days, Mrs Clamp?' I asked.

'Oh, *I'm* well enough,' Mrs Clamp said, shaking her head and coming down off the stool, picking up some more frozen burgers and going back to the freezer. I wondered if she might ever get frostbite; I was sure I could see little crystals of ice glinting on her faint moustache.

'My, that's a big load you've brought for us today. I'm surprised you didn't fall over on the way here.'

'You won't catch *me* falling over, no.' Mrs Clamp shook her head once more, went to the sink, reached up and over while on her tip-toes, turned on the hot water, rinsed her hands, wiped them on her blue-check, bri-nylon work-coat and took some cheese from the bike.

'Can I make you a cup of something, Mrs Clamp?'

'Not for *me*,' Mrs Clamp said, shaking her head inside the fridge, slightly below the height of the ice-making compartment.

'Oh, well, I won't, then.' I watched her wash her hands one more time. While she started sorting out the lettuce from the spinach I took my leave and went up to my room.

We ate our usual Saturday lunch: fish, with potatoes from the garden. Mrs Clamp was at the other end of the table from my father instead of me, as is traditional. I sat halfway down the table with my back to the sink, arranging fish bones in meaningful patterns on the plate while Father and Mrs Clamp exchanged very formal, almost ritualised pleasantries. I made a tiny human skeleton with the bones of the dead fish and distributed a little ketchup about it to make it more realistic.

'More tea, Mr Cauldhame?' Mrs Clamp said.

'No, thank you, Mrs Clamp,' my father replied.

'Francis?' Mrs Clamp asked me.

'No, thank you,' I said. A pea would do for a rather green skull for the skeleton. I placed it there. Father and Mrs Clamp

73

droned on about this and that.

'I hear the constable was down the other day, if you don't mind *me* saying so,' Mrs Clamp said, and coughed politely.

'Indeed,' my father said, and shovelled so much food into his mouth he wouldn't be able to speak for another minute or so. Mrs Clamp nodded at her much-salted fish and sipped her tea. I hummed, and my father glared at me over jaws like heaving wrestlers.

Nothing more was said on the subject.

Saturday night at the Cauldhame Arms and there I stood as usual at the back of the packed, smoke-filled room at the rear of the hotel, a plastic pint glass in my hand full of lager, my legs braced slightly on the floor in front of me, my back against a wallpapered pillar, and Jamie the dwarf sitting on my shoulders, resting his pint of Heavy on my head now and again and engaging me in conversation.

'What you been doin', then, Frankie?'

'Not a lot. I killed a few rabbits the other day and I keep getting weird phone calls from Eric, but that's about all. What about you?'

'Nothin' much. How come Eric's calling you?'

'Didn't you know?' I said, looking up at him. He leaned over and looked down at me. Faces look funny upside down. 'Oh, he's escaped.'

'*Escaped?*'

'Sh. If people don't know, there's no need to tell them. Yeah, he got out. He's called the house a couple of times and he says he's coming this way. Diggs came and told us the day he broke out.'

'Christ. Are they looking for him?'

'So Angus says. Hasn't there been anything on the news? I thought you might have heard something.'

'Nup. Jeez. Do you think they'll tell people in the town if they don't catch him?'

'Don't know.' I would have shrugged.

'What if he's still into setting dogs on fire? Shit. And those worms he used to try to get kids to eat. The locals'll go crazy.' I could feel him shaking his head.

74

'I think they're keeping it quiet. Probably they think they can catch him.'

'Do you think they'll catch him?'

'Ho. I couldn't say. He might be crazy, but he's clever. He wouldn't have got out in the first place if he hadn't been, and when he calls up he sounds sharp. Sharp but bonkers.'

'You don't seem all that worried.'

'I hope he makes it. I'd like to see him again. And I'd like to see him get all the way back here because . . . just because.' I took a drink.

'Shit. I hope he doesn't cause any aggro.'

'He might. That's all I'm worried about. He sounds like he might still not like dogs an awful lot. I think the kids are safe, though, all the same.'

'How's he travelling? Has he told you how he's intendin' to get here? Has he any money?'

'He must have some to be making the phone calls, but he's stealing things mostly.'

'God. Well, at least you can't lose remission for escaping from a loony bin.'

'Ay,' I said. The band came on then, a group of four punks from Inverness called the Vomits. The lead singer had a Mohican haircut and lots of chains and zips. He grabbed the microphone while the other three started thrashing their respective instruments and screamed:

'Ma gurl-fren's leff me an ah feel like a bum,
Ah loss ma job an when ah wank ah can't cum. . . .'

I nestled my shoulders against the pillar a little more firmly and sipped from my glass as Jamie's feet beat against my chest and the howling, crashing music thundered through the sweaty room. This sounded like it would be fun.

During the interval, while one of the barmen was taking a mop and bucket to the front of the stage where everybody had been spitting, I went up to the bar to get some more drinks.

'The usual?' said Duncan behind the bar, Jamie nodded. 'And how's Frank?' Duncan asked, pulling a lager and a

75

Heavy.

'OK. And yourself?' I said.

'Getting along, getting along, You still wanting bottles?'

'No, thanks. I've got enough for my home-brew now.'

'We'll still see you in here, though, will we?'

'Oh, yes,' I said. Duncan reached up to hand Jamie his pint and I took mine, putting the money down at the same time.

'Cheers, lads,' Duncan said as we turned and went back to the pillar.

A few pints later, when the Vomits were doing their first encore, Jamie and I were up dancing, jumping up and down, Jamie shouting and clapping his hands and dancing about on my shoulders. I don't mind dancing with girls when it's for Jamie, though one time with one tall lassie he wanted us both to go outside so he could kiss her. The thought of her tits pressed up against my face nearly made me throw up, and I had to disappoint him. Anyway, most of the punk girls don't smell of perfume and only a few wear skirts and even then they're usually leather ones. Jamie and I got pushed about a bit and nearly fell down a couple of times, but we survived through to the end of the night without any scrapes. Unfortunately, Jamie ended up talking to some woman, but I was too busy trying to breathe deeply and keep the far wall steady really to care.

'Yeah, I'm going to get a bike soon. Two-fifty, of course,' Jamie was saying. I was half-listening. He was not going to get a bike because he wouldn't be able to reach the pedals, but I wouldn't have said anything even if I could have, because nobody expects people to tell the truth to women and, besides, that's what friends are for, as they say. The girl, when I could see her properly, was a rough-looking twenty, and had as many coats of paint over her eyes as a Roller gets on its doors. She smoked a horrible French cigarette.

'Ma mate's got a bike – Sue. It's a Suzuki 185GT her brother used tae have, but she's saving up fur a Gold Wing.'

They were putting the chairs up on the tables and wiping up the mess and the cracked glasses and limp crisp-bags, and I still wasn't feeling too good. The girl sounded worse the more

I listened to her. Her accent sounded horrible: west coast somewhere; Glasgow, I shouldn't wonder.

'Naw, I wouldn't have one of those. Too heavy. A five hundred would do me. I really fancy a Moto Guzzi, but I'm not sure about shaft drive. . . .'

Christ, I was about to do the Technicolor Yawn all over this girl's jacket, through the tears and rusting her zips and filling her pockets, and probably send Jamie flying across the room into the beer-crates under the speaker stacks with the first awful heave, and here were these two trading absurd biker fantasies.

'Want a fag?' the girl said, shoving a packet up past my nose towards Jamie. I was seeing trails and lights from the blue packet's passing even after she brought it back down. Jamie must have taken a cigarette even though I knew he didn't smoke, because I saw the lighter go up, igniting in front of my eyes in a shower of sparks like a fireworks display. I could almost feel my occipital lobe fusing. I thought of making some smart remark to Jamie about stunting his growth, but all lines to and from my brain seemed to be jammed with urgent messages coming from my guts. I could feel an awful churning going on down there, and I was sure it would only end one way, but I couldn't move. I was stuck there like a flying buttress between the floor and the pillar, and Jamie was still gibbering away to the girl about the sound a Triumph makes and the high-speed runs she'd done up the side of Loch Lomond at night.

'You on holiday, like?'

'Aye, me an' ma mates. Ah've got a boyfriend but he's oot on the rigs.'

'Aw aye.'

I was still breathing hard, trying to clear my head with oxygen. I didn't understand Jamie; he was half the size I was, half the weight or less, and no matter how much we drank together he never seemed to be affected. He certainly wasn't dumping his pints on the floor on the sly; I'd have got wet if he was. I realised that the girl had finally noticed me. She poked my shoulder for what I gradually comprehended wasn't the first time.

'Hey,' she said.

'What?' I struggled.

'You all right?'

'Aye,' I nodded slowly, hoping to content her with this, then looked away and up to one side as though I had just found something very interesting and important to look at on the ceiling. Jamie nudged me with his feet. 'What?' I said again, not trying to look at him.

'You staying here all night?'

'What?' I said. 'No. How, are you ready? Right.' I put my hands behind me to find the pillar, found it and pushed myself up, hoping my feet wouldn't slip on the beer-wet floor.

'Maybe you'd better let me down, Frank lad,' Jamie said, nudging me hard. I looked sort of up and to the side again, as though at him, then nodded. I let my back slide down the pillar until I was virtually squatting on the floor. The girl helped Jamie jump down. His red hair and her blonde looked suddenly garish from that angle in the now brightly lit room. Duncan was coming closer with the brush and a big bucket, emptying ashtrays and mopping things. I struggled to get up, then felt Jamie and the girl take me one under each arm and help me. I was starting to get triple vision and wondering how you did that with only two eyes. I wasn't sure if they were talking to me or not.

I said, 'Aye,' just in case they were, then felt myself being led out into the fresh air through the fire exit. I needed to go to the toilet, and with every step I took there seemed to be more convulsions from my guts. I had this horrible vision of my body being made up almost completely of two equal-sized compartments, one holding piss and the other undigested beer, whisky, crisps, dry-roasted peanuts, spit, snot, bile and one or two bits of fish and potatoes. Some sick part of my mind suddenly thought of fried eggs lying thick with grease on a plate, surrounded with bacon, curled and scooped and holding little pools of fat, the outsides of the plate dotted with coagulated lumps of grease. I fought down the ghastly urge coming up from my stomach. I tried to think of *nice* things; then, when I couldn't think of any, I determined to concentrate on what was happening around me. We were

78

outside the Arms, walking along the pavement past the Bank, Jamie on one side of me and the girl on the other. It was a cloudy night and cool, and the streetlights were sodium. We left the smell of the pub behind, and I tried to get some of the fresh air through my head. I was aware I was staggering slightly, lurching sporadically into Jamie or the girl, but there wasn't a great deal I could do about it; I felt rather like one of those ancient dinosaurs so huge that they had a virtually separate brain to control their back legs. I seemed to have a separate brain for each limb, but they'd all broken off diplomatic relations. I swayed and stumbled along as best I could, trusting to luck and the two people with me. Frankly, I didn't have much faith in either, Jamie being too small to stop me if I really started to topple, and the girl being a girl. Probably too weak; and, even if she wasn't, I expected she would just let me crack my skull on the pavement because women like to see men helpless.

'You tae alwiz like rat?' the girl said.

'Like what?' Jamie said, without, I thought, the correct amount of pre-emptive indignation.

'You up on his showders.'

'Oh, no, that's just so I can see the band better.'

'Thank Christ fur 'at. Ah thought maybe ye went tae ra bog like rat.'

'Oh, aye; we go into a cubicle and Frank goes in the bowl while I do it into the cistern.'

'Yur kiddin'!'

'Aye,' Jamie said in a voice distorted by a grin. I was walking along as best I could, listening to all this garbage. I was slightly annoyed at Jamie saying anything, even jokingly, about me going to the toilet; he knows how sensitive I am about it. Only once or twice has he taunted me with what sounds like the interesting sport of going into the gents in the Cauldhame Arms (or anywhere else, I suppose) and attacking the drowned fag-ends in the urinals with a stream of piss.

I admit I have watched Jamie doing this and been quite impressed. The Cauldhame Arms has excellent facilities for the sport, having a great long gutter-like urinal extending right along one wall and halfway down another, with only one drainhole. According to Jamie, the object of the game is to get a soggy fag-end from wherever it is in the channel along to and down the coverless hole, breaking it up as much as possible *en route*. You can score points for the number of ceramic divisions you can move the butt over (with extra for actually getting it down the hole and extra for doing it from the far end of the gutter from the hole), for the amount of destruction caused – apparently it's very hard to get the little black cone at the burned end to disintegrate – and, over the course of the evening, the number of fag-ends so dispatched.

The game can be played in a more limited form in the little bowl-type individual urinals which are more fashionable these days, but Jamie has never tried this himself, being so short that if he is to use one of those he has to stand about a metre back from it and lob his waste water in.

Anyway, it sounds like something to make long pisses much more interesting, but it is not for me, thanks to cruel fate.

'Is he yur bruthur or sumhin?'

'Naw, he's ma friend.'

'Zay olwiz get like iss?'

'Ay, usually, on a Saturday night.'

This is a monstrous lie, of course. I am rarely so drunk that I can't talk or walk straight. I'd have told Jamie as much, too, if I'd been able to talk and hadn't been concentrating on putting one foot in front of the other. I wasn't so sure I was going to throw up now, but that same irresponsible, destructive part of my brain – just a few neurons probably, but I suppose there are a few in every brain and it only takes a very small hooligan element to give the rest a bad name – kept thinking about those fried eggs and bacon on the cold plate, and each time I almost heaved. It took an act of will to think of cool winds on hilltops or the pattern of water-shadows over wave-carved sand – things which I have always thought epitomise clarity and freshness and helped to divert my brain from dwelling on the contents of my stomach.

However, I did need to have a piss even more desparately than before. Jamie and the girl were inches away from me, holding me by an arm each, being bumped into frequently, but my drunkenness had now got to such a state – as the last

80

two quickly consumed pints and an accompanying whisky caught up with my racing bloodstream – that I might as well have been on another planet for all the hope I had of making them understand what I wanted. They walked on either side of me and talked to each other, jabbering utter nonsense as though it was all so important, and I, with more brains than the two of them put together and information of the most vital nature, couldn't get a word out.

There had to be a way. I tried to shake my head clear and take some more deep breaths. I steadied my pace. I thought very carefully about *words* and how you made them. I checked my tongue and tested my throat. I *had* to pull myself together. I had to *communicate*. I looked round as we crossed a road; I saw the sign for Union Street where it was fixed to a low wall. I turned to Jamie and then the girl, cleared my throat and said quite clearly: 'I didn't know if you two ever shared – or, indeed, still do share, for that matter, for all that I know, at least mutually between yourselves but at any rate not including me – the misconception I once perchanced to place upon the words contained upon yonder sign, but it is a fact that I thought the "union" referred to in said nomenclature delineated an association of working people, and it did seem to me at the time to be quite a socialist thing for the town fathers to call a street; it struck me that all was not yet lost as regards the prospects for a possible peace or at the very least a cease-fire in the class war if such acknowledgements of the worth of trade unions could find their way on to such a venerable and important thoroughfare's sign, but I must admit I was disabused of this sadly over-optimistic notion when my father – God rest his sense of humour – informed me that it was the then recently confirmed union of the English and Scottish parliaments the local worthies – in common with hundreds of other town councils throughout what had until that point been an independent realm – were celebrating with such solemnity and permanence, doubtless with a view to the opportunities for profit which this early form of takeover bid offered.'

The girl looked at Jamie. 'Dud he say sumhin er?'

'I thought he was just clearing his throat,' said Jamie.

'Ah thought he said sumhin aboot bananas.'

'*Bananas?*' Jamie said incredulously, looking at the girl.

'Naw,' she said, looking at me and shaking her head. 'Right enough.'

So much for communication, I thought. Obviously both so drunk they didn't even understand correctly spoken English. I sighed heavily as I looked first at one and then at the other while we made our slow way down the main street, past Woolworth and the traffic lights. I looked ahead and tried to think what on earth I was going to do. They helped me over the next road, me nearly tripping as I crossed the far kerb. Suddenly I was very aware of the vulnerability of my nose and front teeth, should they happen to come into contact with the granite of Porteniel's pavements at any velocity above quite a small fraction of a metre per second.

'Aye, me and one of my mates have been going round the Forestry Commission tracks up in the hills, goin' round at fifty, skiddin' all over the place like a speedway.'

'Za'afac'?'

My God, they were still talking about bikes.

'Where-ur we takin' hum own-yway?'

'Ma mum's. If she's still up, she'll make us some tea.'

'Yer *maw's?*'

'Aye.'

'Aw.'

It came to me in a flash. It was so obvious I couldn't imagine why I hadn't seen it before. I knew there was no time to lose and no point in hesitating – I was going to explode soon – so I put my head down and broke free from Jamie and the girl, running off down the street. I'd escape; do an Eric so I could find somewhere nice and quiet for a piss.

'Frank!'

'Aw, fur fuck's sek, gie's a brek, whit's ay up tae noo?'

The pavement was still below my feet, which were moving more or less as they were supposed to. I could hear Jamie and the girl running after me shouting, but I was already past the old chip shop and the war memorial and picking up speed. My distended bladder wasn't helping matters, but it wasn't holding me back as much as I'd feared, either.

'Frank! Come back! Frank, stop! What's wrong? Frank, ya crazy bastard, you'll break your neck!'

'Aw, le'm gaw, zafiez hied.'

'No! He's my friend! *Frank!*'

I turned the corner into Bank Street, pounded down it just missing two lamp-posts, took a sharp left into Adam Smith Street and came to McGarvie's garage. I skidded into the forecourt and ran behind a pump, gasping and belching and feeling my head pound. I dropped my cords and squatted down, leaning back against the five-star pump and breathing heavily as the pool of steaming piss collected on the bark-rough concrete of the fuel apron.

Footsteps clattered and a shadow came from the right of me. I looked round to see Jamie.

'Haw – ha – ha –' he gasped, putting one hand on another pump to steady himself as he bent over a little and looked at his feet, the other hand on a knee, his chest heaving. 'Here – ha – here – ha – here you – ha – are. Fffwwaaw. . . .' He sat down on the plinth supporting the pumps and stared at the dark glass of the office for a while. I sat, too, slumped against the pump, letting the last drops fall free. I stumbled back and sat down heavily on the plinth, then staggered upright and pulled my cords back up.

'What did you do that for?' Jamie said, still panting.

I waved at him, struggling to do my belt up. I was starting to feel sick again, getting magnified wafts of pub smoke off my clothes.

'Saw—' I started to say 'Sorry', then the word turned into a heave. That anti-social part of my brain suddenly thought about the greasy eggs and bacon again and my stomach geysered. I doubled up, retching and heaving, feeling my guts contract like a balling fist inside me; involuntary, alive, like a woman must feel with a kicking child. My throat was rasped with the force of the jet. Jamie caught me as I almost fell over. I stood there like a half-opened penknife, splattering the forecourt noisily. Jamie shoved one hand down the back of my cords to keep me from falling on my face, and put the other hand on to my forehead, murmuring something. I went on being sick, my stomach starting to hurt badly now; my eyes were full of tears, my nose was running and my whole head felt like a ripe tomato, ready to burst. I fought for breath between heaves, snatching down flecks of vomit and coughing and spewing at the same time. I listened to myself make a horrible noise like Eric going crazy over the phone, and hoped that nobody was passing and could see me in such an undignified and weak position. I stopped, felt better, then started again and felt ten times worse. I moved to one side with Jamie helping me and went down on my hands and knees on a comparatively clean part of the concrete where the oil stains looked old. I coughed and spluttered and gagged a few times, then fell back into Jamie's arms, bringing my legs up to my chin to ease the ache in my stomach muscles.

'Better now?' Jamie said. I nodded. I tipped forward so that I rested on both buttocks and heels, my head between my knees. Jamie patted me. 'Just a minute, Frankie lad.' I felt him go off for a few seconds. He came back with some coarse paper towels from the forecourt dispenser and wiped my mouth with one bit and the rest of my face with another bit. He even took them and put them in the litter-bin.

Though I still felt drunk, my stomach ached and my throat felt like a couple of hedgehogs had had a fight in it, I did feel a lot better. 'Thanks,' I managed, and started trying to stand. Jamie helped me to my feet.

'By God, what a state to get yourself in, Frank.'

'Aye,' I said, wiping my eyes with my sleeve and looking round to see that we were still alone. I clapped Jamie on the shoulder a couple of times and we made for the street.

We walked up the deserted street with me breathing deeply and Jamie holding me by one elbow. The girl had gone, obviously enough, but I wasn't sorry.

'Why'd you run off like that?'

I shook my head. 'Needed to go.'

'What?' Jamie laughed. 'Why didn't you just say?'

'Couldn't.'

'Just 'cause there was a girl there?'

'No,' I said, and coughed. 'Couldn't speak. Too drunk.'

'What?' laughed Jamie.

I nodded. 'Yeah,' I said. He laughed again and shook his

head. We kept on walking.

Jamie's mother was still up and she made us some tea. She's a big woman who's always in a green housecoat when I see her in the evenings after the pub when, as often happens, her son and I end up at her house. She's not too unpleasant, even if she does pretend to like me more than I know she really does.

'Och, laddie, you're not looking your best. Here, sit down and I'll get some tea on the go. Ach, you wee lamb.' I was planted in a chair in the living-room of the council house while Jamie hung up our jackets. I could hear him jumping in the hall.

'Thank you,' I croaked, throat dry.

'There you are, pet. Now, do you want me to turn on the fire for you? Are you too cold?'

I shook my head, and she smiled and nodded and patted me on the shoulder and padded off to the kitchen. Jamie came in and sat on the couch next to my chair. He looked at me and grinned and shook his head.

'What a state. What a *state!*' He clapped his hands and rocked forward on the couch, his feet sticking out straight in front of him. I rolled my eyes and looked away. 'Never mind, Frankie lad. A couple of cups of tea and you'll be fine.'

'Huh,' I managed, and shivered.

I left about one o'clock in the morning, more sober, and awash with tea. My stomach and throat were almost back to normal, though my voice still sounded harsh. I bade Jamie and his mother goodnight and walked on through the outskirts of town to the track heading for the island, then down the track in blackness, sometimes using my small torch, towards the bridge and the house.

It was a quiet walk through the marsh and dune land and the patchy pasture. Apart from the few noises I made on the path, all I could hear was the very occasional and distant roar of heavy trucks on the road through town. The clouds covered most of the sky and there was little light from the moon, and none ahead of me at all.

I remembered once, in the middle of summer two years ago, when I was coming down the path in the late dusk after a day's

85

walking in the hills beyond the town, I saw in the gathering night strange lights, shifting in the air over and far beyond the island. They wavered and moved uncannily, glinting and shifting and burning in a heavy, solid way no thing should in the air. I stood and watched them for a while, training my binoculars on them and seeming, now and again in the shifting images of light, to discern structures around them. A chill passed through me then and my mind raced to reason out what I was seeing. I glanced quickly about in the gloom, and then back to those distant, utterly silent towers of flickering flame. They hung there in the sky like faces of fire looking down on the island, like something waiting.

Then it came to me, and I knew.

A mirage, a reflection of layers on air out to sea. I was watching the gas-flares of oil-rigs maybe hundreds of kilometres away, out in the North Sea. Looking again at those dim shapes around the flame, they did appear to be rigs, vaguely made out in their own gassy glare. I went on my way happy after that – indeed, happier than I had been before I had seen the strange apparitions – and it occurred to me that somebody both less logical and less imaginative would have jumped to the conclusion that what they had seen were UFOs.

I got to the island eventually. The house was dark. I stood looking at it in the darkness, just aware of its bulk in the feeble light of a broken moon, and I thought it looked even bigger than it really was, like a stone-giant's head, a huge moonlit skull full of shapes and memories, staring out to sea and attached to a vast, powerful body buried in the rock and sand beneath, ready to shrug itself free and disinter itself on some unknowable command or cue.

The house stared out to sea, out to the night, and I went into it.

5: A Bunch of Flowers

I KILLED little Esmerelda because I felt I owed it to myself
and to the world in general. I had, after all, accounted for two
male children and thus done womankind something of a
statistical favour. If I really had the courage of my
convictions, I reasoned, I ought to redress the balance at least
slightly. My cousin was simply the easiest and most obvious
target.

Again, I bore her no personal ill-will. Children aren't real
people, in the sense that they are not small males and females
but a separate species which will (probably) grow into one or
the other in due time. Younger children in particular, before
the insidious and evil influence of society and their parents
have properly got to them, are sexlessly open and hence
perfectly likeable. I did like Esmerelda (even if I thought her
name was a bit soppy) and played with her a lot when she came
to stay. She was the daughter of Harmsworth and Morag
Stove, my half-uncle and half-aunt by my father's first

marriage; they were the couple who had looked after Eric between the ages of three and five. They would come over from Belfast to stay with us in the summers sometimes; my father used to get on well with Harmsworth, and because I looked after Esmerelda they could have a nice relaxing holiday here. I think Mrs Stove was a little worried about trusting her daughter to me that particular summer, as it was the one after I'd struck young Paul down in his prime, but at nine years of age I was an obviously happy and well-adjusted child, responsible and well-spoken and, when it was mentioned, demonstrably sad about my younger brother's demise. I am convinced that only my genuinely clear conscience let me convince the adults around me that I was totally innocent. I even carried out a double-bluff of appearing slightly guilty *for the wrong reasons,* so that adults told me I shouldn't blame myself because I hadn't been able to warn Paul in time. I was brilliant.

I had decided I would try to murder Esmerelda before she and her parents even arrived for their holiday. Eric was away on a school cruise, so there would only be me and her. It would be risky, so soon after Paul's death, but I had to do something to even up the balance. I could feel it in my guts, in my bones; I *had* to. It was like an itch, something I had no way of resisting, like when I walk along a pavement in Porteneil and I accidentally scuff one heel on a paving stone. I *have* to scuff the other foot as well, with as near as possible the same weight, to feel good again. The same if I brush one arm against a wall or a lamp-post; I must brush the other one as well, soon, or at the very least scratch it with the other hand. In a whole range of ways like that I try to keep balanced, though I have no idea why. It is simply something that must be done; and, in the same way, I had to get rid of *some* woman, tip the scales back in the other direction.

I had taken to making kites that year. It was 1973, I suppose. I used many things to make them: cane and dowling and metal coathangers and aluminium tent-poles, and paper and plastic sheeting and dustbin bags and sheets and string and nylon rope and twine and all sorts of little straps and buckles and bits of cord and elastic bands and strips of wire and pins and screws and nails and pieces cannibalised from model yachts and various toys. I made a hand winch with a double handle and a ratchet and room for half a kilometre of twine on the drum; I made different types of tails for the kites that needed them, and dozens of kites large and small, some stunters. I kept them in the shed and eventually had to put the bikes outside under a tarpaulin when the collection got too large.

That summer I took Esmerelda kiting quite a lot. I let her play with a small, single-string kite while I used a stunter. I would send it swooping over and under hers, or dive it down to the sands while I stood on a dune cliff, pulling the kite down to nick tall towers of sand I'd built, then pulling up again, the kite trailing a spray of sand through the air from the collapsing tower. Although it took a while and I crashed a couple of times, once I even knocked a dam down with a kite. I swooped it so that on each pass it caught the top of the dam wall with one corner, gradually producing a nick in the sand barrier which the water was able to flow through, quickly going on to overwhelm the whole dam and the sand-house village beneath.

Then one day I was standing there on a dune top, straining against the pull of the wind in the kite, gripping and hauling and sensing and adjusting and twisting, when one of those twists became like a strangle around Esmerelda's neck, and the idea was there. Use the kites.

I thought about it calmly, still standing there as though nothing had passed through my mind but the continual computation guiding the kite, and I thought it seemed reasonable. As I thought about it, the notion took its own shape, blossoming, as it were, and escalating into what I finally conceived as my cousin's nemesis. I grinned then, I recall, and brought the stunter down fast and acute across the weeds and the water, the sand and the surf, scudding it in across the wind to jerk and zoom just before it hit the girl herself where she sat on the dune top holding and spasmodically jerking the string she held in her hand, connected to the sky. She turned, smiled and shrieked then, squinting in the summer light. I laughed, too, controlling the thing in the skies above and the thing in the brain beneath, equally well.

I built a big kite.

It was so big it didn't even fit inside the shed. I made it from old aluminium tent-poles, some of which I had found in the attic a long time previously and some I had got from the town dump. The fabric, at first, was black plastic bags, but later became tent fabric, also from the attic.

I used heavy orange nylon fishing-line for the string, wound round a specially made drum for the winch, which I had strengthed and fitted with a chest-brace. The kite had a tail of twisted magazine-pages – *Guns and Ammo*, which I got regularly at the time. I painted the head of a dog on the canvas in red paint because I had yet to learn I was not a Canis. My father had told me years before that I was born under the starsign of the Dog because Sirius was overhead at the time. Anyway, that was just a symbol.

I went out very early one morning, just after the sun came up and long before anybody else woke. I went to the shed, got the kite, walked a way along the dunes and assembled it, battered a tent-peg into the ground, tied the nylon to it, then flew the kite on a short string for a while. I sweated and strained with it, even in quite a light wind, and my hands grew warm despite the heavy-duty welding-gloves I had on. I decided the kite would do, and brought it in.

That afternoon, while the same wind, now freshened, still blew across the island and off into the North Sea, Esmerelda and I went out as usual, and stopped off at the shed to pick up the dismantled kite. She helped me carry it far along the dunes, dutifully clutching the lines and winch to her flat little chest and clicking the ratchet on the drum, until we reached a point well out of sight from the house. It was a tall dune head stuck nodding towards distant Norway or Denmark, grass like hair swept over the brow and pointing.

Esmerelda searched for flowers while I constructed the kite with an appropriately solemn slowness. She talked to the flowers, I recall, as though trying to persuade them to show themselves and be collected, broken and bunched. The wind blew her blonde hair in front of her face as she walked, squatted, crawled and talked, and I assembled.

Finally the kite was finished, fully made up and lying like a collapsed tent on the grass, green on green. The wind coursed over it and flapped it – little whip noises that stirred it and made it seem alive, the dog-face scowling. I sorted the orange nylon lines out and did some tying, untangling line from line, knot from knot.

I called Esmerelda over. She had a fistful of tiny flowers, and made me wait patiently while she described them all, making up her own names when she forgot or had never learned the real ones. I accepted the daisy she gave me graciously and put it in the buttonhole of my jacket's left breast pocket. I told her that I had finished constructing the new kite, and that she could help me test it in the wind. She was excited, wanting to hold the strings. I told her she might get a chance, though of course I would have the ultimate control. She wanted to hold the flowers as well, and I told her that might just be possible.

Esmerlda ooh'd and ah'd over the size of the kite and the fierce doggy painted on it. The kite lay on the wind-ruffled grass like an impatient manta, rippling. I found the main control lines and gave them to Esmerelda, showing her how to hold them, and where. I had made loops to go over her wrists, I told her, so that she wouldn't lose her grip. She struck her hands through the braided nylon, holding one line tight and grasping the posy of bright flowers and the second line with her other hand. I got my part of the control lines together and carried them in a loop round to the kite. Esmerelda jumped up and down and told me to hurry up and make the kite fly. I took a last look round, then only had to kick the top edge of the kite up a little for it to take the wind and lift. I ran back behind my cousin while the slack between her and the rapidly ascending kite was taken up.

The kite blew into the sky like something wild, hoisting its tail with a noise like tearing cardboard. It shook itself and cracked in the air. It sliced its tail and flexed its hollow bones. I came up behind Esmerelda and held the lines just behind her little freckled elbows, waiting for the tug. The lines came taut, and it came. I had to dig my heels in to stay steady. I

bumped into Esmerelda and made her squeal. She had let the
lines go when the first brutal snap had straightened the nylon,
and stood glancing back at me and staring up into the sky as I
fought to control the power in the skies above us. She still
clutched the flowers, and my tuggings on the lines moved her
arms like a marionette, guided by the loops. The winch rested
against my chest, a little slack between it and my hands.
Esmerelda looked round one last time at me, giggling, and I
laughed back. Then I let the lines go.

The winch hit her in the small of the back and she yelped.
Then she was dragged off her feet as the lines pulled her and
the loops tightened round her wrists. I staggered back, partly
to make it look good on the offchance there was somebody
watching and partly because letting go of the winch had put
me off balance. I fell to the ground as Esmerelda left it forever.
The kite just kept snapping and flapping and flapping and
snapping and it hauled the girl off the earth and into the air,
winch and all. I lay on my back and watched it for a second,
then got up and ran after her as fast as I could, again just
because I knew I couldn't catch her. She was screaming and
waggling her legs for all she was worth, but the cruel loops of
nylon had her about the wrists, the kite was in the jaws of the
wind, and she was already well out of reach even if I had
wanted to catch her.

I ran and ran, jumping off a dune and rolling down its
seaward face, watching the tiny struggling figure being
hoisted farther and farther into the sky as the kite swept her
away. I could just barely hear her yells and shouts, a thin
wailing carried on the wind. She sailed over the sands and the
rocks and out towards the sea, me running, exhilarated,
underneath, watching the stuck winch bob under her kicking
feet. Her dress billowed out around her.

She went higher and higher and I kept running, outpaced
now by the wind and the kite. I ran through the ripple-puddles
at the margins of the sea, then into it, up to my knees. Just
then something, at first seemingly solid, then separating and
dissociating, fell from her. At first I though she had pissed
herself, then I saw flowers tumble out of the sky and hit the
water ahead of me like some strange rain. I waded out over the

92

shallows until I came to them, and gathered the ones I could, looking up from my harvest as Esmerelda and kite struck out for the North Sea. It did cross my mind that she might actually get across the damn thing and hit land before the wind dropped, but I reckoned that even if that happened I had done my best, and honour was satisfied.

I watched her get smaller and smaller, then turned and headed for shore.

I knew that three deaths in my immediate vicinity within four years *had* to look suspicious, and I had already planned my reaction carefully. I didn't run straight home to the house, but went back up into the dunes and sat down there, holding the flowers. I sang songs to myself, made up stories, got hungry, rolled around in the sand a bit, rubbed a little of it into my eyes and generally tried to psyche myself up into something that might look like a terrible state for a wee boy to be in. I was still sitting there in the early evening, staring out to sea when a young forestry worker from the town found me.

He was one of the search party drummed up by Diggs after my father and relations missed us and couldn't find us and called the police. The young man came over the tops of the dunes, whistling and casually whacking clumps of reed and grass with a stick.

I didn't take any notice of him. I kept staring and shivering and clutching the flowers. My father and Diggs came along after the young man passed word along the line of people beating their way along the dunes, but I didn't take any notice of those two, either. Eventually there were dozens of people clustered around me, looking at me, asking me questions, scratching their heads, looking at their watches and gazing about. I didn't take any notice of them. They formed their line again and started searching for Esmerelda while I was carried back to the house. They offered me soup I was desperate for but took no notice of, asked me questions I answered with a catatonic silence and a stare. My uncle and aunt shook me, their faces red and eyes wet, but I took no notice of them. Eventually my father took me to my room, undressed me and put me to bed.

Somebody stayed in my room all night and, whether it was

my father, Diggs or anybody else, I kept them and me awake all night by lying quiet for a while, feigning sleep, then screaming with all my might and falling out of bed to thrash about on the floor. Each time I was picked up, cuddled and put back to bed. Each time I pretended to go to sleep again and went crazy after a few minutes. If any of them talked to me, I just lay shaking in the bed staring at them, soundless and deaf.

I kept that up until dawn, when the search party returned, Esmerelda-less, then I let myself go to sleep.

It took me a week to recover, and it was one of the best weeks of my life. Eric came back from his school cruise and I started to talk a little after he arrived; just nonsense at first, then later disjointed hints at what had happened, always followed by screaming and catatonia.

Sometime around the middle of the week, Dr MacLennan was allowed to see me for a while, after Diggs overruled my father's refusal to have me medically inspected by anybody else but him. Even so, he stayed in the room, glowering and suspicious, making sure that the examination was kept within certain limits; I was glad he didn't let the doctor look all over me, and I responded by becoming a little more lucid.

By the end of the week I was still having the occasional fake nightmare, I would suddenly go very quiet and shivery every now and again, but I was eating more or less normally and could answer most questions quite happily. Talking about Esmerelda, and what had happened to her, still brought on mini-fits and screams and total withdrawal for a while, but after long and patient questioning by my father and Diggs I let them know what I wanted them to think had happened – a big kite; Esmerelda becoming entangled in the lines; me trying to help her and the winch slipping out of my fingers; desperate running; then a blank.

I explained that I was afraid I was jinxed, that I brought death and destruction upon all those near me, and also that I was afraid I might get sent to prison because people would think I had murdered Esmerelda. I wept and I hugged my father and I even hugged Diggs, smelling his hard-blue uniform fabric as I did so and almost feeling him melt and believe me. I asked him to go to the shed and take all my kites away and burn them, which he duly did, in a hollow now called Kite Pyre Dell. I was sorry about the kites, and I knew that I'd have to give up flying them for good to keep the act looking realistic, but it was worth it. Esmerelda never did show up; nobody saw her after me, as far as Diggs' enquiries of trawlers and drilling-rigs and so on could show.

So I got to even up the score and have a wonderful, if demanding, week of fun acting. The flowers that I had still been clutching when they carried me back to the house had been prised from my fingers and left in a plastic bag on top of the fridge. I discovered them there, shrivelled and dead, forgotten and unnoticed, two weeks later. I took them for the shrine in the loft one night, and have them to this day, little brown twists of dried plant like old Sellotape, stuck in a little glass bottle. I wonder sometimes where my cousin ended up; at the bottom of the sea, or washed on to some craggy and deserted shore, or blown on to a high mountain face, to be eaten by gulls or eagles. . . .

I would like to think that she died still being floated by the giant kite, that she went round the world and rose higher as she died of starvation and dehydration and so grew less weighty still, to become, eventually, a tiny skeleton riding the jetstreams of the planet; a sort of Flying Dutchwoman. But I doubt that such a romantic vision really matches the truth.

I spent most of Sunday in bed. After my binge of the previous night, I wanted rest, lots of liquid, little food, and my hangover to go away. I felt like deciding then and there never to get drunk again, but being so young I decided that this was probably a little unrealistic, so I determined not to get *that* drunk again.

My father came and banged at my door when I didn't appear for breakfast.

'And what's wrong with you, as if I need ask?'

'Nothing,' I croaked at the door.

'That'll be right,' my father said sarcastically. 'And how much did you have to drink last night?'

'Not much.'

'Hnnh,' he said.

'I'll be down soon,' I said, and rocked to and fro in the bed to make noises which might make it sound as though I was getting up.

'Was that you on the phone last night?'

'What?' I asked the door, stopping my rocking.

'It was, wasn't it? I thought it was you; you were trying to disguise your voice. What were you doing ringing at that time?'

'Aah . . . I don't remember ringing, Dad, honest,' I said carefully.

'Hnnh. You're a fool, boy,' he said, and clumped off down the hall. I lay there, thinking. I was quite sure I hadn't called the house the previous night. I had been with Jamie in the pub, then with him and the girl outside, then alone when I was running, and then with Jamie and later him and his mother, then I walked home almost sober. There were no blank spots. I assumed it must have been Eric calling. From the sound of it my father couldn't have spoken to him for very long, or he would have recognised his son's voice. I lay back in my bed, hoping that Eric was still at large and heading this way, and also that my head and guts would stop reminding me how uncomfortable they could feel.

'Look at you,' my father said when I eventually came down in my dressing-gown to watch an old movie on the television that afternoon. 'I hope you're proud of yourself. I hope you think feeling like that makes you a man.' My father tutted and shook his head, then went back to reading the *Scientific American*. I sat down carefully in one of the lounge's big easy chairs.

'I did get a bit drunk last night, Dad, I admit it. I'm sorry if it upsets you, but I assure you I'm suffering for it.'

'Well, I hope that teaches you a lesson. Do you realise how many brain cells you probably managed to kill off last night?'

'A good few thousand,' I said after a brief pause for calculation.

My father nodded enthusiastically: 'At least.'

'Well, I'll try not to do it again.'

'Hnnh.'

'Br*rap*!' said my anus loudly, surprising me as well as my father. He put the magazine down and stared into space over my head, smiling wisely as I cleared my throat and flapped the hem of my dressing-gown as unobtrusively as I could. I could see his nostrils flex and quiver.

'Lager and whisky, eh?' he said, nodding to himself and taking up his magazine again. I felt myself blush and I gritted my teeth, glad he had retreated behind the glossy pages. How did he *do* that? I pretended nothing had happened.

'Oh. By the way,' I said, 'I hope you don't mind, but I told Jamie that Eric had escaped.'

My father glared over the magazine, shook his head and continued reading. 'Idiot,' he said.

In the evening, after a snack rather than a meal, I went up to the loft and used the telescope to take a distant look at the island, making sure that nothing had happened to it while I rested inside the house. Everything appeared calm. I did go for one short walk in the cool overcast, just along the beach to the south end of the island and back, then I stayed in and watched some more television when the rain came on, carried on a low wind, glummuttering against the window.

I had gone to bed when the phone rang. I got up quickly, as I hadn't really started to drop off when it went, and ran down to get there before my father. I didn't know if he was still up or not.

'Yes?' I said breathlessly, tucking my pyjama jacket into the bottoms. Pips sounded, then a voice on the other end sighed.

'No.'

'What?' I said, frowning.

'No,' the voice on the other end said.

'Eh?' I said. I wasn't even sure it was Eric.

'You said "Yes". I say "No".'

'What do you want me to say?'

'"Porteneil 531."'

'OK. Porteneil 531. Hello?'

'OK. Goodbye.' The voice giggled, the phone went dead. I

looked at it accusingly, then put it down in the cradle. I hesistated. The phone rang again. I snatched it up halfway through the first tinkle.

'Ye—' I started, then the pips sounded. I waited until they stopped and said; 'Porteneil 531.'

'Porteneil 531,' said Eric. I thought it was Eric, at least.

'Yes,' I said.

'Yes what?'

'Yes, this is Porteneil 531.'

'But I thought *this* was Porteneil 531.'

'*This* is. Who is that ? Is that you—'

'It's me. Is that Porteneil 531?'

'Yes!' I shouted.

'And who's that?'

'Frank Cauldhame,' I said, trying to be calm. 'Who's that?'

'Frank Cauldhame,' Eric said. I looked around, up and down the stairs, but saw no sign of my father.

'Hello, Eric,' I said, smiling. I decided that, whatever else happened, tonight I would not make him angry. I'd put the phone down rather than say the wrong thing and have my brother wreck yet another piece of Post Office property.

'I just told you my name's Frank. Why are you calling me "Eric"?'

'Come on, Eric, I recognise your voice.'

'I'm Frank. Stop calling me Eric.'

'OK. OK. I'll call you Frank.'

'So who are you?'

I thought for a moment. 'Eric?' I said tentatively.

'You just said you were called Frank.'

'Well,' I sighed, leaning against the wall with one hand and wondering what I could say. 'That was . . . that was just a joke. Oh God, I don't know.' I frowned at the phone and waited for Eric to say something.

'Anyway, Eric,' Eric said, 'what's the latest news?'

'Oh, nothing much. I was out last night, at the pub. Did you call last night?'

'Me? No.'

'Oh. Dad said somebody did. I thought it might have been you.'

'Why would I call?'

'Well, I don't know.' I shrugged to myself. 'For the same reason you called tonight. Whatever.'

'Well, why do you think I called tonight?'

'I don't know.'

'Christ; you don't know why I've called, you aren't sure of your own name, you get mine wrong. You're not up to much, are you?'

'Oh dear,' I said, more to myself than to Eric. I could feel this conversation going all the wrong way.

'Aren't you going to ask me how *I* am?'

'Yes, yes,' I said. 'How are you?'

'Terrible. How are you?'

'OK. Why are you feeling terrible?'

'You don't really care.'

'Of course I care. What's wrong?'

'Nothing that would interest you. Ask me something else, like how the weather is or where I am or something. I know you don't care how I feel.'

'Of course I do. You're my brother. Naturally I care,' I protested. Just at that moment I heard the kitchen door open, and seconds later my father appeared at the bottom of the stairs and, taking hold of the great wooden ball sculpted on to the top of the last banister, stood glaring up at me. He lifted his head and put it slightly to one side to listen better. I missed a little of what Eric said in reply to me, and only caught;

' . . . care how I feel. Every time I ring up it's the same. "Where are you?" That's all you care about; you don't care about where my head's at, only my body. I don't know why I bother, I don't. I might as well not take the trouble of calling.'

'H'm. Well. There you are,' I said, looking down at my father and smiling. He stood there, silent and unmoving.

'See what I mean? That's all you can say. "H'm. Well. There you are." Thanks a fucking lot. That shows all you care.'

'Not at all. Quite the contrary,' I told him, then put the phone just a little away from my mouth and shouted to my father: 'It's only Jamie again, *Dad*!'

' . . . why I bother to make the effort really I don't. . . ,'

Eric rambled on in the earpiece, apparently oblivious to what I'd just said. My father ignored it, too, standing in the same position as before, head cocked.

I licked my lips and said; 'Well, Jamie—'

'What? You see? You've forgotten my name again now. What's the use? That's what I'd like to know. H'm? What's the use? *He* doesn't love me. *You* love me, though, don't you, h'm?' His voice became slightly fainter and more echoey; he must have taken his mouth away from the handset. It sounded as though he was talking to somebody else in the call-box with him.

'Yes, Jamie, of course.' I smiled at my father and nodded and put one hand under the other armpit, trying to look as relaxed as possible.

'You love me, don't you, my sweet? As though your little heart was on fire for me . . .,' Eric mumbled far away. I swallowed and smiled again at my father.

'Well, that's the way things go, Jamie. I was just saying that to *Dad here* this morning.' I waved at Father.

'You're burning up with love for me, aren't you, me little darlin'?'

My heart and stomach seemed to collide as I heard a rapid panting noise come over the phone behind Eric's muttering. A slight whine and some slobbering noises brought goose-pimples up all over me. I shivered. My head shook as though I'd just knocked back some hundred-proof whisky. Pant pant whine whine went the noise. Eric said something soothing and quiet in the background. Oh my God, he had a dog in there with him. Oh, no.

'Well! Listen! Listen, Jamie! What do you think?' I said loudly and desperately, wondering if my father could see my goosebumps. I thought my eyes must be starting out of my head, too, but there was little I could do; I was trying the best I could to think of something distracting to say to Eric. 'I was – ah – I was just thinking that we really must – must get Willy to give us another shot of his old car; you know, the Mini he bombs up and down the sands on sometimes? That was really good fun earlier on, wasn't it?' I was croaking by now, my mouth drying up.

100

'What? What are you talking about?' Eric's voice said suddenly, close to the phone again. I swallowed, smiled once more at my father, whose eyes seemed to have narrowed slightly.

'You remember, Jamie. Getting a shot of Willy's Mini. I really must get *Dad here*' – I hissed those two words – 'to get me an old car I could drive on the sands.'

'You're talking crap. I've never driven anybody's car on the sands. You've forgotten who I am again,' Eric said, still not listening to what I was saying. I turned away from looking down at my father and faced into the corner, sighing mightily and whispering 'Oh my God,' to myself, away from the mouthpiece.

'Yes. Yes, that's right, Jamie,' I continued hopelessly. 'That brother of mine is still making his way here, as far as I can tell. Me and *Dad here* are hoping he's all right.'

'You little bastard! You're talking as though I'm not even here! *Christ*, I hate when people do that! *You* wouldn't do that to me, would you, me old flame?' His voice went away again, and I heard doggy noises – puppy noises, come to think of it – over the phone. I was starting to sweat.

I heard footsteps in the hall below, then the kitchen light click off. The footsteps came again, then started up the stairs. I turned round quickly, smiled at my father as he approached.

'Well, there you go, Jamie,' I said pathetically, drying up metaphorically as well as literally.

'Don't spend too long on that phone,' my father said as he passed me, and continued up the stairs.

'Right, Dad!' I shouted merrily, beginning to experience an ache somewhere near my bladder that I sometimes get when things are going particluarly badly and I can't see any way out.

'*Aaaaoooo!*'

I jerked the phone away from my ear and stared into it for a second. I couldn't decide whether Eric or the dog had made the noise.

'Hello? Hello?' I whispered feverishly, glancing up to see Father's shadow leave the wall on the floor above.

'Haaaooo*wwwaaaaooooww*!' came the scream down the line. I shook and flinched. My God, what was he *doing* to the

101

animal? Then the receiver clunked, I heard a shout like a curse, and the phone rattled and crashed again. 'You little bastard— Aargh! Fuck! Shit. Come back, you little—'

'Hello! Eric! I mean Frank! I mean— Hello! What's happening?' I hissed, glancing up the stairs for shadows, crouching down at the phone and covering up my mouth with my free hand. 'Hello?'

There was a clatter, then 'That was your fault!' shouted close to the handset, then another crash. I could hear vague noises for a bit, but even straining I couldn't make out what they were, and they could have been just noises on the line. I wondered whether I should put the phone down, and was about to do so when Eric's voice came again, muttering something I couldn't make out.

'Hello? What?' I said.

'Still there, eh? I lost the little bastard. That was your fault. Christ, what's the use of you?'

'I'm sorry,' I said, genuinely.

'Too bloody late now. Bit me, the little shit. I'll catch it again, though. Bastard.' The pips went. I heard more money being put in. 'I suppose you're glad, aren't you?'

'Glad what?'

'Glad the goddam *dog* got away, asshole.'

'What? Me?' I stalled.

'You aren't trying to tell me you're *sorry* it got away, are you?'

'Ah. . . .'

'You did it on purpose!' Eric shouted. 'You did it on purpose! You wanted it to get away! You won't let me play with anything! You'd rather the dog enjoyed itself than me! You shit! You rotten bastard!'

'Ha ha,' I laughed unconvincingly. 'Well, thanks for calling – ah – Frank. Goodbye.' I slammed the receiver down and stood for a second, congratulating myself on how well I had done, all things considered. I wiped my brow, which had become a little sweaty, and took a last look up at the shadowless wall above.

I shook my head and trudged up the stairs. I'd got as far as the top step on that flight when the phone went again. I froze.

102

If I answered it. . . . But if I didn't, and father did. . . .

I ran back down, picked it up, heard the coins go in; then *'Bastard!'* followed by a series of deafening crashes as plastic met metal and glass. I closed my eyes and listened to the cracks and smashes until one especially loud thump ended in a low buzz telephones don't usually make; then I put the phone down again, turned, looked upward, and set wearily off, back up the stairs.

I lay in bed. Soon I would have to try some long-range fixing of this problem. It was the only way. I'd have to try to influence things through the root cause of it all: Old Saul himself. Some heavy medicine was required if Eric wasn't to wreck single-handedly the entire Scottish telephone network and decimate the country's canine population. First, though, I would have to consult the Factory again.

It wasn't exactly my fault, but I was totally involved, and I might just be able to do something about it, with the skull of the ancient hound, the Factory's help and a little luck. How susceptible my brother would be to whatever vibes I could send out was a question I didn't like too much to think about, given the state of his head, but I had to do something.

I hoped the little puppy *had* got well away. Dammit, *I* didn't hold all dogs to blame for what had happened. Old Saul was the culprit, Old Saul had gone down in our history and my personal mythology as the Castraitor, but thanks to the little creatures who flew the creek I had him in my power now.

Eric was crazy all right, even if he was my brother. He was lucky to have somebody sane who still liked him.

6: The Skull Grounds

WHEN Agnes Cauldhame arrived, eight and a half months pregnant, on her BSA 500 with the swept-back handlebars and eye of Sauron painted red on the petrol-tank, my father was, perhaps understandably, not ferociously pleased to see her. She had, after all, deserted him almost immediately after my birth, leaving him holding the squealing baby. To disappear without so much as a phone call or a postcard for three years and then breeze back down the path from the town and across the bridge – rubber handlebars just clearing the sides and no more – carrying somebody else's baby or babies and expecting to be housed, fed, nursed and delivered by my father was a little presumptuous.

Being only three at the time, I can't remember much about it. In fact I can't remember anything about it at all, just as I can't remember anything before the age of three. But then, of course, I have my own good reasons for that. From the little I've been able to piece together when my father has chosen to let slip some information, I've been able to get what I think is an accurate idea of what happened. Mrs Clamp has come across with some details on sporadic occasions, too, though they are probably no more to be relied on than what my father's told me.

Eric was away at the time, staying with the Stoves in Belfast.

Agnes, tanned, huge, all beads and bright caftan, determined to give birth in the lotus position (in which she claimed the child had been conceived) while going 'Om', refused to answer any of my father's questions about where she had been for the three years and who she had been with. She told him not to be so possessive about her and her body. She was well and with child; that was all he needed to know.

Agnes ensconced herself in what had been their bedroom despite my father's protests. Whether he was secretly glad to have her back, and perhaps even had some foolish idea that she might be back to stay, I can't say. I don't think he is all that forceful really, despite the aura of brooding presence he can show when he wants to be impressive. I suspect that my mother's obviously determined nature would have been enough to master him. Anyway, she got her way, and lived in fine style for a couple of weeks that heady summer of love and peace, etcetera.

My father still had full use of both his legs at the time, and had to use them to run up and down from kitchen or lounge to the bedroom and back when Agnes rang the little bells sewn into the bell-bottoms of her jeans, which lay draped over a chair by the side of the bed. On top of that, my father had to look after me. I was toddling around at the time getting into mischief the way any normal, healthy three-year-old boy does.

As I say, I can't remember anything, but I'm told that I did seem to enjoy annoying Old Saul, the bandy-legged and ancient white bulldog my father kept – I'm told – because it was so ugly and it didn't like women. It didn't like motorbikes, either, and had gone wild when Agnes first arrived, barking and attacking. Agnes kicked it across the garden and it ran off yelping into the dunes, only reappearing once Agnes was

105

safely out of the way, confined to bed. Mrs Clamp maintains that my father ought to have put the dog down years before all this happened, but I think the wet-jowled, yellow-bleary-eyed, fishy-smelling old hound must have worked on his sympathy just by being so repulsive.

Agnes duly went into labour about lunch-time one hot still day, pouring sweat and Omming to herself while my father boiled lots of water and things and Mrs Clamp dabbed Agnes's brow and like as not told her of all the women she'd known who had died in childbirth. I played outside, running around in a pair of shorts and – I imagine – quite happy to have the whole pregnancy thing going on because it gave me more freedom to do as I liked about the house and garden, free from my father's supervision.

What I ever did to annoy Old Saul, whether it was the heat that made him especially cantankerous, whether Agnes really had kicked him in the head when she arrived, as Mrs Clamp says – none of this do I know. But the little tousle-headed, dirty, tanned, bold toddler that was me might well have been up to some sort of mischief involving the beast.

It happened in the garden, over a piece of ground that later became a vegetable patch when my father went on his health-food binge. My mother was heaving and grunting, pushing and breathing, an hour or so away from producing, and attended by both Mrs Clamp and my father, when all three (or at least two; I suppose Agnes might have been too preoccupied) heard frenzied barking and one high, awful scream.

My father rushed to the window, looked out and down into the garden, then shouted and ran out of the room, leaving Mrs Clamp goggle-eyed, alone.

He ran out into the garden and picked me up. He ran back into the house, shouted up to Mrs Clamp, then put me on the table in the kitchen and used some towels to stop the bleeding as best he could. Mrs Clamp, still ignorant and quite enraged, appeared with the medicine he had demanded, then almost fainted when she saw the mess between my legs. My father took the bag from her and told her to get back upstairs to my mother.

106

One hour later I had recovered consciousness, was lying drugged and bloodless in my bed, and my father had gone out with the shotgun he owned then to look for Old Saul.

He found him in a couple of minutes, before he had properly left the house. The old dog was cowering by the door of the cellar, down the steps in the cool shadow. He whined and shivered, and my young blood mixed on his slavering chops with gamey saliva and thick eye-mucus as he girned and looked shakily and pleadingly up at my father, who picked him up and strangled him.

Now, I did eventually get my father to tell me this; and, according to him, it was just as he choked the last struggling life out of the dog that he heard another scream, this time from above, and inside the house, and that was the boy they called Paul being born. What sort of twisted thoughts went through my father's brain at the time to make him choose such a name for the child I cannot start to imagine, but that was the name Angus chose for his new son. He had to choose it by himself because Agnes didn't stay long. She spent two days recovering, expressed shock and horror at what had happened to me, then got on her bike and roared off. My father tried to stop her by standing in her way, so she ran him over and broke his leg quite badly, on the path before the bridge.

Thus it was that Mrs Clamp found herself looking after my father while he insisted on looking after me. He still refused to let the old woman call in any other doctor, and set his own leg, though not quite perfectly; hence the limp. Mrs Clamp had to take the newly born child into the local cottage hospital the day after Paul's mother left. My father protested but, as Mrs Clamp pointed out, it was quite enough to have to look after two invalids in the one house without having an infant needing constant care as well.

So that was my mother's last visit to the island and the house. She left one dead, one born and two crippled for life, one way or the other. Not a bad score for a fortnight in the summer of groovy and psychedelic love, peace and general niceness.

Old Saul ended up buried in the slope behind the house, in what later I called the Skull Grounds. My father claims that he cut the animal open and found my tiny genitals in its stomach, but I never did get him to tell me what he did with them.

Paul, of course, was Saul. That enemy was – must have been – cunning enough to transfer to the boy. That was why my father chose such a name for my new brother. It was just lucky that I spotted it in time and did something about it at such an early age, or God knows what the child might have turned into, with Saul's soul possessing him. But luck, the storm and I introduced him to the Bomb, and that settled his game.

As for the little animals, the gerbils, white mice and hamsters, they had to die their muddy little ploppy deaths so that I could get to the Skull of Old Saul. I catapulted the tiny beasts across the creek and into the mud on the far side so that I could have funerals. My father would never have let me start digging up our graveyard for family pets otherwise, so off they had to go, departing this life in the rather undignified garb of half a badminton shuttlecock. I used to buy the shuttlecocks in the town toy and sports shop and cut the rubber end off, then squeeze the protesting guinea-pig (I did use one once, just on principle, but as a rule they were too expensive and a little too big) up through the funnel of plastic until it sat round their waist like a little dress. Thus flighted, I sent them shooting out over the mud and the water towards their suffocating ends; then I buried them, using as coffins the big matchboxes we always kept by the stove, and which I had been saving for years and using as toy-soldier containers, model houses and so on.

I told my father I was trying to get them over to the far side, to the mainland, and that the ones I had to bury, the ones which fell short, were victims of scientific research, but I doubt I really needed this excuse; my father never seemed bothered about the suffering of lower forms of life, despite having been a hippy, and perhaps because of his medical training.

I kept a log, naturally, and therefore have it recorded that it took no less than thirty-seven of these supposed flight experiments before my trusty long-handled trowel, in biting the Skull Grounds' earth skin, struck something harder than the sandy soil, and I finally knew where the dog's bones were.

It would have been nice if it had been a decade to the day since the dog died that I exhumed its skull, but in fact I was a few months late. Nevertheless, the Year of the Skull ended with my old enemy in *my* power; the bone jug pulled from the ground like a very rotten tooth indeed one suitably dark and stormy night, by torchlight and Stoutstroke the trowel while my father was sleeping and I should have been, and the heavens shook with thunder, rain and gale.

I was shaking by the time I got the thing to the Bunker, nearly frightening myself to death with my paranoid imaginings, but I prevailed; I took the filthy skull there and I cleaned it and stuck a candle in it and I surrounded it with heavy magic, important things, and got back cold and wet to my warm little bed safely.

So, all things considered, I think I have done all right, handled my problem as well as it could have been handled. My enemy is twice dead, and I *still* have him. I am not a full man, and nothing can ever alter that; but I am me, and I regard that as compensation enough.

This burning dogs stuff is just nonsense.

7: Space Invaders

BEFORE I realised the birds were my occasional allies, I used to do unkind things to them: fish for them, shoot them, tie them to stakes at low tide, put electrically detonated bombs under their nests, and so on.

My favourite game was capturing two using bait and a net, then tying them together. Usually they were gulls and I tied thick orange nylon fishing-line to a leg each, then sat on a dune and watched. Sometimes I would have a gull and a crow but, whether they were the same species or not, they quickly found out they couldn't fly properly – though the twine was long enough in theory – and ended up (after a few hilariously clumsy aerobatics) fighting.

With one dead, though, the survivor – usually injured – wasn't really any better off, attached to a heavy corpse instead of a live opponent. I have seen a couple of determined ones peck the leg off their defeated adversary, but most were unable, or didn't think of it, and got caught by the rats during the night.

I had other games, but that one always struck me as one of my more mature inventions; symbolic somehow, and with a nice blend of callousness and irony.

One of the birds shat on Gravel as I pedalled up the path to town on the Tuesday morning. I stopped, glared up at the wheeling gulls and a couple of thrushes, then got some grass and wiped the yellow-white mess off the front guard. It was a bright, sunny day and a light breeze blew. The forecast for the next few days was good, and I hoped the fine weather held for Eric's arrival.

I met Jamie in the lounge bar of the Cauldhame Arms for lunch and we sat playing an electronic game over a TV table.

'If he's that crazy, I don't know why they haven't caught him yet,' Jamie said.

'I've told you; he's crazy but he's very cunning. He's not *stupid*. He was always very bright, right from the start. He was reading early and getting all his relations and uncles and aunts to say "Och, they're old so young these days" and things like that before I was even born.'

'But he is insane, all the same.'

'That's what *they* say, but I don't know.'

'What about the dogs? And the maggots?'

'OK, that looks pretty crazy, I'll admit, but sometimes I think maybe he's up to something, maybe he's not really crazy after all. Perhaps he just got fed up acting normal and decided to act crazy instead, and they locked him up because he went too far.'

'And he's mad at them,' Jamie grinned, drinking his pint as I annihilated various dodging, multi-coloured spacecraft on the screen. I laughed. 'Yeah, if you like. Oh, I don't know. Maybe he really is crazy. Maybe I am. Maybe everybody is. Or at least all of my family.'

'*Now* you're talking.'

I looked up at him for a second, then smiled. 'It does occur to me sometimes. My dad's an eccentric . . . I suppose I am, too.' I shrugged, concentrated on the space battle again. 'But it doesn't bother me. There are a lot madder people about the place.'

Jamie sat in silence for a while as I went from screenful to screenful of wheeling, whining craft. Finally my luck ran out and they caught me. I took up my pint as Jamie settled in to blast a few of the gaudy formations. I looked at the top of his head as he bent to the task. He was starting to go bald, though I knew he was only twenty-three. He reminded me again of a puppet, with his out-of-proportion head and stubby little arms and legs waggling with the exertion of punching the 'fire' button and jiggling the positioning joystick.

'Yeah,' he said after a while, still attacking the oncoming craft, 'and a lot of them seem to be politicians and presidents and things.'

'What?' I said, wondering what he was talking about.

'The madder people. A lot of them seem to be leaders of countries or religions or armies. The real loonies.'

'Aye, I suppose.' I said thoughtfully, watching the battle on the screen upside down. 'Or maybe they're the only sane ones. After all, they're the ones with all the power and riches. They're the ones who get everybody else to do what they want them to do, like die for them and work for them and get them into power and protect them and pay taxes and buy them toys, and they're the ones who'll survive another big war, in their bunkers and tunnels. So, given things being the way they are, who's to say they're the loonies because they don't do things the way Joe Punter thinks they ought to be done? If they thought the same way as Joe Punter, they'd *be* Joe Punter, and somebody else would be having all the fun.'

'Survival of the fittest.'

'Yeah.'

'Survival of the –' Jamie drew his breath in sharply and pulled the stick so hard he almost fell off his stool, but he managed to dodge the darting yellow bolts that had driven him into the corner of the screen ' – nastiest.' He looked up at me and grinned quickly before hunching over the controls again. I drank, nodded.

'If you like. If the nastiest survive, then that's our tough shit.'

'"Us" being all us Joe Punters,' Jamie said.

112

'Aye, or everybody. The whole species. If we're really so bad and so thick that we'd actually use all those wonderful H-bombs and *Neutron* bombs on each other, then maybe it's just as well we do wipe ourselves out before we can get into space and start doing horrible things to other races.'

'You mean we'll be the Space Invaders?'

'Yeah!' I laughed, and rocked back on my stool. 'That's it! That's really us!' I laughed again and tapped the screen above a formation of red and green flapping things, just as one of them, peeling off to the side of the main pack, dived down firing at Jamie's craft, missing it with its shots but clipping him with one green wing as it disappeared off the bottom of the screen, so that Jamie's craft detonated in a blaze of flashing red and yellow.

'Shit,' he said, sitting back. He shook his head.

I sat forward and waited for my craft to appear.

Just a little drunk on my three pints, I cycled back to the island whistling. I always enjoyed my lunch-time chats with Jamie. We sometimes talk when we meet on Saturday nights, but we can't hear when the bands are on, and afterwards I'm either too drunk to talk or, if I can speak, I'm too drunk to recall much of what I've said. Which, come to think of it, is probably just as well, judging by the way people who are normally quite sensible dissolve into gibbering, rude, opinionated and bombastic idiots once the alcohol molecules in their blood-stream outnumber their neurons, or whatever. Luckily, one only notices this if one stays sober oneself, so the solution is as pleasant (at the time, at least) as it is obvious.

My father was asleep in a deckchair in the front garden when I got back. I left the bike in the shed and watched him from the shed door for a while, poised so that if he happened to wake up it would look as though I was just in the act of shutting the door. His head was tilted a little to me and his mouth was slightly open. He had dark glasses on, but I could just see through them to his closed eyes.

I had to go for a piss, so I didn't watch him for very long. Not that I had any particular reason for watching him; I just liked doing it. It made me feel good to know that I could see

113

him and he couldn't see me, and that I was aware and fully conscious and he wasn't.

I went into the house.

I had spent Monday, after a cursory check of the Poles, making one or two repairs and improvements to the Factory, working through the afternoon until my eyes got sore and my father had to call up to me to come down for my dinner.

In the evening it rained, so I had stayed in and watched television. I went to bed early. Eric didn't call.

After I'd got rid of about half the beer I'd drunk in the Arms, I went to have another look at the Factory. I clambered up into the loft, all sunlight and warmth and smelling of old and interesting books, and I decided to clear the place up a bit.

I sorted out old toys into boxes, got a few rolls of carpet and wallpaper back into their places from where they'd fallen, pinned a couple of maps back on to the sloping wooden under-roof, cleared away some of the tools and bits and pieces that I'd used to repair the Factory, and loaded the various sections of the Factory that needed to be loaded.

I found some interesting things while I was doing all this: a home-made astrolabe I'd carved, a box containing the folded-flat parts for a scale model of the defences around Byzantium, the remains of my collection of telegraph-pole insulators, and some old jotters from when my father was teaching me French. Leafing through them, I couldn't see any obvious lies; he hadn't taught me to say anything obscene instead of 'Excuse me' or 'Can you direct me to the railway station, please?', though I'd have thought the temptation would have been all but irresistible.

I completed tidying the loft, sneezing a few times as the golden space filled with motes of shining dust. I looked over the refurbished Factory again, just because I love looking at it and tinkering with it and touching it and tipping some of its little levers and doors and devices. Finally I dragged myself away, telling myself that I'd get a chance to use it properly soon enough. I would capture a fresh wasp that afternoon to use the following morning. I wanted another interrogation

114

of the Factory before Eric arrived; I wanted more of an idea what was going to happen.

It was a little risky, of course, asking it the same question twice, but I thought the exceptional circumstances demanded it, and it was my Factory, after all.

I got the wasp without any difficulty. It more or less walked into the ceremonial jam-jar which I have always used to hold subjects for the Factory. I kept the jar, sealed with the lid with the holes in it and stocked with a few leaves and a morsel of orange peel, standing in the shade of the river bank while I made a dam there that afternoon.

I worked and sweated in the sunlight of late afternoon and early evening while my father did a bit of painting at the back of the house and the wasp felt its way around the inside of the jar, antennae waving.

Halfway through building the dam – not the best time – I thought it might be amusing to make it an Exploder, so I set the overflow going and trotted up the path to the shed for the War Bag. I brought it back and sorted out the smallest bomb I could find wired for electrical detonation. I attached it to the wires from the torch-firer by the bared ends poking out of the drilled hole in the black metal casing and wrapped the bomb in a couple of plastic bags. I shoved the bomb backwards into the base of the main dam, leading the wires away and back behind the dam, past the static waters backed up behind it to near where the wasp crawled in its jar. I covered the wires over so that it looked more natural, then went on building the dam.

The dam system ended up very big and complicated and included not one but two little villages, one between two of the dams and one downstream from the last one. I had bridges with little roads, a small castle with four towers, and two road tunnels. Just before tea-time I played out the last of the wire from the torch body and took the wasp jar up on to the top of the nearby dune.

I could see my father, still painting the window surrounds of the lounge. I can just remember the designs he used to have on the front of the house, the face turned towards the sea; they were fading even then, but they were minor classics of

tripped-out art, as I recall; great sweeping sworls and
mandalas that leaped about the house front like Technicolor
tattoos, curving round windows and arching over the door. A
relic from the days when my father was a hippy, they are worn
and gone now, erased by wind and sea and rain and sunlight.
Only the vaguest outlines are still discernible now, along with
a few freak patches of real colour, like peeling skin.

I opened the torch-firer up, shoved the cylindrical batteries
inside, secured them, then clicked the flasher button on top of
the torch body. The current flowed in series with the nine-volt
pack-battery taped to the outside, down the wires leading
from the hole where the bulb used to go, and into the casing of
the bomb. Somewhere near its centre, steel wool glowed
dully, then brightly and started to melt, and the white crystal
mixture exploded, tearing the metal – which it took me and a
heavy-duty vice a lot of sweat, time and leverage to bend at all
– as though it was paper.

Wham! The front of the main dam crashed up and out; a
messy mix of steam and gas, water and sand leaped into the air
and fell back spattering. The noise was good and dull, and the
tremor I felt through the seat of my pants just before I heard
the whump, single and strong.

The sand in the air slipped, fell back, splashed in the waters
and thudded in little heaps on to roads and houses. The
unleashed waters flooded out of the gap smashed in the sand
wall and rolled down, sucking sand from the edges of the
breach and spilling in a sloped brown tide down upon the first
village, cutting through it, piling up behind the next dam,
backing up, collapsing sand houses, tipping the castle to one
side as a unit and undermining its already cracked towers. The
bridge supports gave way, the wood slipped, fell in at one side,
then the dam started to spill over and soon its whole top was
awash and being eaten away by the flood still piling out of the
first dam as the head of water pushed forward from fifty
metres or more back up the stream. The castle disintegrated,
falling over.

I left the jar and ran down the dune, exulting in the wave of
water as it sped over the braided surface of the stream bed, hit
houses, followed roads, ran through tunnels, then hit the last

116

dam, quickly overwhelmed it and went on to smash into the rest of the houses, grouped into the second village. Dams were disintegrating, houses slipping into the water, bridges and tunnels falling and banks collapsing all over the place; a gorgeous feeling of excitement rose in my stomach like a wave and settled in my throat as I thrilled to the watery havoc about me.

I watched the wires wash and roll themselves to one side of the flood's course, then looked at the front of the racing water as it headed quickly for the sea over the long-dried sand. I sat down opposite where the first village had been, where long brown humps of water surged, slowly advancing, and waited for the storm of water to subside, my legs crossed, my elbows on my knees and my face in my hands. I felt warm and happy and slightly hungry.

Eventually, when the stream was almost back to normal and there was virtually nothing left of my hours of work, I spotted what I was looking for: the black and silver wreck of the bomb, sticking ripped and gnarled in the sand just downstream from the site of the dam it had destroyed. I didn't take my boots off but, with the tips of my toes still on the dry bank, walked with my hands until I was almost at full stretch out in the middle of the stream. I picked the remains of the bomb out of the stream bed, put its jagged body carefully into my mouth, then walked my hands back until I was able to throw myself back and stand up.

I wiped the almost flat piece of metal with a rag from the War Bag, put the bomb inside the bag, then collected the wasp jar and went back to the house for tea, leaping the stream just up from the highest point the waters had been backed up to.

All our lives are symbols. Everything we do is part of a pattern we have at least some say in. The strong make their own patterns and influence other people's, the weak have their courses mapped out for them. The weak and the unlucky, and the stupid. The Wasp Factory is part of the pattern because it is part of life and – even more so – part of death. Like life it is complicated, so all the components are there. The reason it can answer questions is because every question is a start looking for an end, and the Factory is about the End – death, no less. Keep your entrails and sticks and dice and books and birds and voices and pendants and all the rest of that crap; I have the Factory, and it's about now and the future; not the past.

I lay in bed that night, knowing the Factory was primed and ready and waiting for the wasp that crawled and felt its way about the jar that lay by my bedside. I thought of the Factory, above me in the loft, and I waited for the phone to ring.

The Wasp Factory is beautiful and deadly and perfect. It would give me some idea of what was going to happen, it would help me to know what to do, and after I had consulted it I would try to contact Eric through the skull of Old Saul. We are brothers, after all, even if only half so, and we are both men, even if I am only half so. At some deep level we understand each other, even though he is mad and I am sane. We even had that link I had not thought of until recently, but which might come in useful now: we have both killed, and used our heads to do it.

It occurred to me then, as it has before, that that is what men are really *for*. Both sexes can do one thing specially well; women can give birth and men can kill. We – I consider myself an honorary man – are the harder sex. We strike out, push through, thrust and take. The fact that it is only an analogue of all this sexual terminology I am capable of does not discourage me. I can feel it in my bones, in my uncastrated genes. Eric must respond to that.

Eleven o'clock came, then midnight and the time signal, so I turned the radio off and went to sleep.

8: The Wasp Factory

IN THE EARLY morning, while my father slept and the cold light filtered through the sharp overcast of young cloud, I rose silently, washed and shaved carefully, returned to my room, dressed slowly, then took the jar with the sleepy-looking wasp in it up to the loft, where the Factory waited.

I left the jar on the small altar under the window and made the last few preparations the Factory required. Once that was done I took some of the green cleaning jelly from the pot by the altar and rubbed it well into my hands. I looked at the Time, Tide and Distance Tables, the little red book that I kept on the other side of the altar, noting the time of high tide. I set the two small wasp candles into the positions the tips of the hands of a clock would have occupied on the face of the Factory if showing the time of local high tide, then I slid the top off the jar a little and extracted the leaves and the small piece of orange peel, leaving the wasp in there alone.

I set the jar on the altar, which was decorated with various

119

powerful things; the skull of the snake which killed Blyth (tracked down and sliced in half by his father, using a garden spade – I retrieved it from the grass and hid that front part of the snake in the sand before Diggs could take it away for evidence), a fragment of the bomb which had destroyed Paul (the smallest bit I could find; there were lots), a piece of tent fabric from the kite which had elevated Esmerelda (not a piece of the actual kite of course, but an off-cut) and a little dish containing some of the yellow, worn teeth of Old Saul (easily pulled).

I held my crotch, closed my eyes and repeated my secret catechisms. I could recite them automatically, but I tried to think of what they meant as I repeated them. They contained my confessions, my dreams and hopes, my fears and hates, and they still make me shiver whenever I say them, automatic or not. One tape recorder in the vicinity and the horrible truth about my three murders would be known. For that reason alone they are very dangerous. The catechisms also tell the truth about who I am, what I want and what I feel, and it can be unsettling to hear yourself described as you have thought of yourself in your most honest and abject moods, just as it is humbling to hear what you have thought about in your most hopeful and unrealistic moments.

Once I had gone through this I took the wasp without further ado to the underside of the Factory, and let it in.

The Wasp Factory covers an area of several square metres in an irregular and slightly ramshackle tangle of metal, wood, glass and plastic. It is all based around the face of the old clock which used to hang over the door of the Royal Bank of Scotland in Porteneil.

The clock face is the most important thing I have ever recovered from the town dump. I found it there during the Year of the Skull and rolled it home down the path to the island and rumbled it over the footbridge. I stored it in the shed until my father was away for the day, then I strained and sweated all day to get it up into the loft. It is made of metal and is nearly a metre in diameter; it is heavy and almost unblemished; the numerals are in roman script and it was

120

made along with the rest of the clock in Edinburgh in 1864, one hundred years exactly before my birth. Certainly not a coincidence.

Of course, as the clock looked both ways, there must have been another face, the other side of the clock; but, although I scoured the dump for weeks after I found the face I do have, I never did discover the other one, so that it, too, is part of the mystery of the Factory – a little Grail legend of its own. Old Cameron in the ironmonger's shop in the town told me that he heard a scrap-metal dealer from Inverness took the workings of the clock, so perhaps the other face was melted down years ago, or now adorns the wall of some smart house on the Black Isle built from the profits of dead cars and the varying price of lead. I'd rather the former.

There were a few holes in the face which I soldered up, but I left the hole in the dead centre where the mechanism connected with the hands, and it is through that the wasp is let into the Factory. Once there it can wander about the face for as long as it likes, inspecting the tiny candles with its dead cousins buried inside if it likes, or ignoring them if it would rather.

Having made its way to the edge of the face, though, where I have sealed it with a wall of plywood two inches high, topped with a metre-circle of glass I had the glazier in the town make specially, the wasp can enter one of twelve corridors through little wasp-sized doors, one opposite each of those – to the wasp – vast numerals. If the Factory so chooses, the weight of the wasp trips a delicate see-saw trigger made from thin pieces of tin can, thread and pins, and a tiny door closes behind the insect, confining it to the corridor it has chosen. Despite the fact that I keep all the door mechanisms well oiled and balanced, and repair and test them until the slightest tremor sets them off – I have to tread very lightly when the Factory is doing its slow and deadly work – sometimes the Factory does not want the wasp in its first choice of corridor, and lets it crawl back out on to the face again.

Sometimes the wasps will fly, or crawl upside down on the bottom of the circle of glass, sometimes they stay a long time by the closed-off hole in the centre through which they enter,

121

but sooner or later they all choose a hole and a door which work, and their fate is sealed.

Most of the deaths the Factory has to offer are automatic, but some do require my intervention for the *coup de grâce*, and that, of course, has some bearing on what the Factory might be trying to tell me. I must pull the trigger on the old air-gun, if the wasp crawls down it; I must turn on the current if it falls into the Boiling Pool. If it ends up crawling into the Spider's Parlour or the Venus Cave or the Antery, then I can just sit and watch nature take its course. If its path takes it to the Acid Pit or the Ice Chamber or the rather jocularly named Gents (where the instrument of ending is my own urine, usually quite fresh), then again I can merely observe. If it falls into the many charged spikes of the Volt Room, I can watch the insect get zapped; if it trips the Deadweight, I can watch it get crushed and ooze; and, if it stumbles through to the Blade Corridor, I can see it chopped and writhe. When I have some of the alternative deaths attached I can watch it tip molten wax over itself, see it eat poisoned jam or be skewered on a pin propelled by a rubber band; it can even set off a chain of events which ought to end with it trapped in a sealed chamber blasted by carbon dioxide from a soda-syphon bulb, but if it should choose either the hot water or the rifled length of the Twist of Fate, then I have to take a direct part in its death. And, if it goes for the Fiery Lake, it is me who has to press the rod which flicks the lighter which ignites the petrol.

Death by fire has always been at Twelve, and it is one of the Ends never replaced by one of the Alternatives. I have signified Fire as Paul's death; that happened near to midday, just as Blyth's exit by venom is represented by the Spider's Parlour at Four. Esmerelda probably died by drowning (the Gents), and I put her time of death arbitrarily at Eight, to keep things symmetrical.

I watched the wasp come up out of the jar, under a photograph of Eric I had placed face down on the glass. The insect wasted no time; it was up on the face of the Factory in seconds. It crawled over the maker's name and the year the clock was born, ignored the wasp candles totally, and went more or less straight for the big XII, over that and through the door opposite, which snicked quietly closed behind it. It went at a fast crawl down the corridor, through the lobster-pot funnel made from thread which would stop it from turning back, then entered the highly polished steel funnel and slipped down into the glass-covered chamber where it would die.

I sat back then, sighing. I pushed a hand through my hair and leaned forward again, watching the wasp where it had fallen as it clambered about the blackened and rainbow-coloured bowl of steel mesh which had been sold as a tea-strainer but now hung over a bowl of petrol. I smiled ruefully. The chamber was well ventilated with many small holes in the metal top and bottom of the glass tube, so that the wasp would not choke on the petrol fumes; a slight odour of petrol could usually be sensed when the Factory was primed, if you put your mind to it. I could smell that petrol as I watched the wasp, and perhaps there was just a trace of drying paint in the atmosphere, too, though I couldn't be sure. I shrugged to myself and pushed down on the chamber button, so that a length of dowling slid down its guide of aluminium tent-pole and came into contact with the wheel and gas-release mechanism on top of the disposable lighter poised over the pool of petrol.

It didn't even need a few tries to catch; it went first time, and the thin flames, still quite bright in the early gloom of the morning-lit loft, curled and licked about the open mesh of the strainer. The flames did not go through, but the heat did, and the wasp flew up, buzzing angrily above the silent flames, bumping against the glass, falling back, hitting the side of the strainer, going over the edge, starting to fall into the flames, then flying back up again, knocking off the steel tube of the funnel a few times, then falling back into the steel-mesh trap. It leaped up a final time, flew hopelessly for a few seconds, but its wings must have been singed, because it was crazily erratic in its flight and soon fell into the gauze bowl and died there, struggling, then curling, then staying still, smoking slightly.

I sat and watched the blackened insect bake and crisp, sat and watched the calm flames rise to the mesh and fan round it like a hand, sat and watched the reflection of the little quivering flames on the far side of the glass tube, then at last

123

reached over, unclipped the base of the cylinder, slid the petrol-dish toward me under a metal cover and snuffed the fire. I undid the top of the chamber and reached in with a pair of tweezers to remove the body. I placed it in a matchbox and put that on the altar.

The Factory does not always give up its dead; the acid and the ants leave nothing, and the Venus fly-trap and the spider give back only a husk, if anything. Again, though, I had a burned body; again I would have to do some disposing. I put my head in my hands, rocking forward on the small stool. The Factory surrounded me, the altar was at my back. I gazed round the Factory's paraphernalia of places, its many ways to death, its crawlways and corridors and chambers, its lights at the ends of tunnels, its tanks and containers and hoppers, its triggers, its batteries and threads, supports and stands, tubes and wires. I clicked a few switches, and tiny propellers whirred down branch-corridors, sending air sucked down vents over thimblefuls of jam and down towards the face. I listened to them for a while, until I could smell jam myself, but that was to tempt slow wasps to their ends, and not for me. I turned the motors off.

I started switching everything off; disconnecting, emptying and feeding. The morning was growing stronger in the space beyond the skylights, and I could hear a couple of early birds calling in the new fresh air. When the ritual standing-down of the Factory was completed I went back to the altar, looking round it at all its parts, the assortment of miniature plinths and small jars, the souvenirs of my life, the previous things I've found and kept. Photographs of all my dead relations, the ones I've killed and the ones that just died. Photographs of the living: Eric, my father, my mother. Photographs of things; a BSA 500 (not *the* bike, unfortunately; I think my father destroyed all the photographs of it), the house when it was still bright with swirling paint, even a photograph of the altar itself.

I passed the matchbox containing the dead wasp over the altar, waved it around in front of it, before the jar of sand from the beach outside, the bottles of my precious fluids, a few shavings from my father's stick, another matchbox with a couple of Eric's first teeth set in cotton wool, a phial with some of my father's hair, another with some rust and paint scraped from the bridge to the mainland. I lit wasp candles, closed my eyes, held the matchbox coffin in front of my forehead so that I could feel the wasp in there from inside my head; an itching, tickling sensation just inside my skull. After that I blew the candles out, covered the altar, stood up, dusted down my cords, took up the photograph of Eric I'd placed on the glass of the Factory and wrapped the coffin in it, secured it with a rubber band and put the package in my jacket pocket.

I walked slowly along the beach towards the Bunker, my hands in my pockets, my head down, watching the sand and my feet but not really watching them. Everywhere I turned there was fire. The Factory had said it twice, I had turned to it instinctively when attacked by the rogue buck, and it was squeezed into every spare corner of my memory. Eric brought it closer all the time, too.

I brought my face up to the sharp air and the pastel blues and pink of the new sky, feeling the damp breeze, hearing the hiss of the distant, outgoing tide. Somewhere a sheep bleated.

I had to try Old Saul, I had to make the attempt to contact my mad, crazy brother before these many fires conjoined and swept Eric away, or swept my life on the island away. I tried to pretend to myself that it might not really be that serious, but I knew in my bones it was; the Factory does not lie, and for once it had been comparatively specific. I was worried.

In the Bunker, with the wasp's coffin resting in front of Old Saul's skull and the light coming out through the sockets of his long-dried eyes, I knelt in the pungent darkness before the altar, head bowed. I thought of Eric; I remembered him as he was before he had his unpleasant experience, when, although he had been away from the island, he was still really part of it. I remembered him as the clever, kind, excitable boy he had been, and I thought of what he was now: a force of fire and disruption approaching the sands of the island like a mad angel, head swarming with echoing screams of madness and delusion.

I leaned forward and put my right hand palm down on the top of the old dog's cranium, keeping my eyes closed. The candle was not long lit, and the bone was only warm. Some unpleasant, cynical part of my mind told me that I looked like Mr Spock in *Star Trek,* doing a mind-meld or whatever, but I ignored it; that didn't matter anyway. I breathed deeply, thought more deeply. Eric's face swam in front of me, freckles and sandy hair and anxious smile. A young face, thin and intelligent and young, the way I thought of him when I tried to remember him when he was happy, during our summers together on the island.

I concentrated, pressured my guts and held my breath, as though I was trying to force a turd out when constipated; the blood roared in my ears. With my other hand I used forefinger and thumb to press my closed eyes into my own skull while my other hand grew hot on Old Saul's. I saw lights, random patterns like spreading ripples or huge fingerprints, swirling.

I felt my stomach clench itself involuntarily and a wave of what felt like fiery excitement swept up from it. Only acids and glands, I knew, but I felt it transport me, from one skull through another to another. Eric! I was getting through! I could feel him; feel the aching feet, the blistered soles, the quivering legs, the sweat-stuck grimy hands, the itching, unwashed scalp; I could smell him as myself, see through those eyes that hardly closed and burned in his skull, raw and shot with blood, blinking drily. I could feel the remains of some awful meal lying dead in my stomach, taste burned meat and bone and fur on my tongue; I was there! I was—

A blast of fire crashed out at me. I was thrown back, slammed away from the altar like a piece of soft shrapnel and bounced off the earth-covered concrete floor to come to rest by the far wall, my head buzzing, my right hand aching. I fell over to one side and curled up around myself.

I lay breathing deeply for a while, hugging my sides and rocking very slightly, my head scraping on the floor of the Bunker. My right hand felt as though it was the size and colour of a boxing-glove. With every slowing beat of my heart it sent a pulse of pain up my arm. I crooned to myself and slowly sat up, rubbing my eyes and still rocking very slightly, my knees

126

and head coming a little closer, drawing slightly back. I tried to nurse my battered ego back to health.

Across the Bunker, as the dim view swam back to focus, I could see the skull still glowing, the flame still burning. I glared at it and brought my right hand up, started licking it. I looked to see if my flight across the floor had damaged anything but as far as I could see everything was in its place; only I had been affected. I gave a shivery sigh and relaxed, letting my head rest on the cool concrete of the wall behind me.

I leaned forward after a while and placed the palm of my hand, still throbbing, on the floor of the Bunker, letting it cool. I kept it there for a while, then brought it up and wiped some of the soil off it, squinting to see if there was any visible damage, but the light was too poor. I got slowly to my feet and went to the altar. I lit the side candles with shaking hands, put the wasp with the rest in the plastic rack to the left of the altar and burned its temporary coffin on the metal plate in front of Old Saul. Eric's photograph took flame, the boyish face disappearing in fire. I blew through one of Old Saul's eyes and put the candle out.

I stood for a moment, collecting my thoughts, then went to the metal door of the Bunker and opened it. The silky light of a cloud-bright morning flooded in and made me grimace. I turned back, put out the other candles and took another look at my hand. The palm was red and inflamed. I licked it again.

Almost I had succeeded. I was sure I had had Eric in my grasp, had his mind there under my hand and been part of him, seen the world through his eyes, heard his blood pump in his head, felt the ground beneath his feet, smelled his body and tasted his last meal. But he had been too much for me. The conflagration in his head was just too strong for anybody sane to cope with. It had a lunatic strength of total commitment about it which only the profoundly mad are continually capable of, and the most ferocious soldiers and most aggressive sportsmen able to emulate for a while. Every particle of Eric's brain was concentrated on his mission of returning and setting fire, and no normal brain – not even mine, which was far from normal and more powerful than most – could match that marshalling of forces. Eric was committed to Total War, a Jihad; he was riding the Divine Wind to at least his own destruction, and there was nothing I could do about it this way.

I locked up the Bunker and went back along the beach to the house, my head down again and even more thoughtful and troubled than I had been on the outward journey.

I spent the rest of the day in the house, reading books and magazines, watching television, and thinking all the time. I could not do anything about Eric from the inside, so I had to change the direction of my attack. My personal mythology, with the Factory behind it, was flexible enough to accept the failure it had just suffered and use such a defeat as a pointer to the real solution. My advance troops had had their fingers burned, but I still had all my other resources. I would prevail, but not through the direct application of my powers. At least, not through the direct application of any other power but imaginative intelligence, and that, ultimately, was the bedrock for everything else. If it could not meet the challenge that Eric represented, then I deserved to be destroyed.

My father was still painting, hauling his way up ladders to windows with the paint-tin and brush clenched between his teeth. I offered to help, but he insisted on doing it himself. I had used the ladders myself several times in the past when I was trying to find a way into my father's study, but he had special locks on the windows, and even kept the blinds down and curtains drawn. I was glad to see the difficulty he had making his way up the ladder. He'd never make it up into the loft. It crossed my mind that it was just as well the house was the height it was, or he might just have been able to climb a ladder to the roof and be able to see through the skylights into the loft. But we were both safe, our mutual citadels secure for the foreseeable future.

For once my father let me make the dinner, and I made a vegetable curry we would both find acceptable while watching an Open University programme on geology on the portable television, which I had taken through to the kitchen for the purpose. Once the business with Eric was over, I decided, I really must restart my campaign to persuade my father to get a VTR. It was too easy to miss good programmes on fine days.

After our meal my father went into town. This was unusual, but I didn't ask why he was going. He looked tired after his day spent climbing and reaching, but he went up to his room, changed into his town clothes, and came limping back into the lounge to bid me farewell.

'I'll be off, then,' he said. He looked round the lounge as though searching for some evidence I had started some heinous mischief already, before he had even left. I watched the TV and nodded without looking at him.

'Right you are,' I said.

'I won't be late. You don't have to lock up.'

'OK.'

'You'll be all right, then?'

'Oh, yes.' I looked at him, crossed my arms and settled deeper into the old easy chair. He stepped back, so that both feet were in the hall and his body was canted into the lounge, only his hand on the door-knob stopping him from falling in. He nodded again, the cap on his head dipping once.

'Right. I'll see you later. See you behave yourself.'

I smiled and looked back to the screen. 'Yes, Dad. See you.'

'Hnnh,' he said, and with one last look round the lounge, as if still checking for vanished silver, he closed the door and I heard him clicking down the hall and out the front door. I watched him go up the path, sat for a while, then went up and tested the door to the study, which, as usual, as always, was so firm it might as well have been part of the wall.

I had fallen asleep. The light outside was waning, some awful American crime series was on the television, and my head was sore. I blinked through gummed eyes, yawned to unstick my lips and get some air into my stale-tasting mouth. I yawned and stretched, then froze; I could hear the telephone.

I leaped out of the seat, stumbled, almost fell, then got to the door, the hall, the stairs and finally the phone as quickly as I could. I lifted the receiver with my right hand, which hurt. I pressed the phone to my ear.

'Hello?' I said.

'Hi, Frankie lad, how's it goin'?' said Jamie. I felt a mixture of relief and disappointment. I sighed.

'Ah, Jamie. OK. How are you?'

'Off work. Dropped a plank on my foot this morning and it's all swollen.'

'Nothing too serious, though?'

'Naw. I'll get the rest of the week off if I'm lucky. I'm goin' to see the doctor tomorrow for a sick line. Just thought I'd let you know I'll be at home during the day. You can bring me grapes sometime if you want.'

'OK. I'll come round maybe tomorrow. I'll give you a call first to let you know.'

'Great. Any more word from you-know-who?'

'Nup. I thought that might have been him when you called.'

'Aye, I thought you might think that. Don't worry about it. I haven't heard of anything strange happening in the town, so he probably isn't here yet.'

'Yeah, but I want to see him again. I just don't want him to start doing all the daft things he did before. I know he'll have to go back, even if he doesn't, but I'd like to see him. I want both things, know what I mean?'

'Yeah, yeah. It'll be OK. I think it'll all be all right in the end. Don't worry about it.'

'I'm not.'

'Good. Well, I'm off to buy a few pints of anaesthetic down the Arms. Fancy comin' along?'

'No, thanks. I'm pretty tired. I was up early this morning. I might see you tomorrow.'

'Great. Well, take care an' that. See you, Frank.'

'Right, Jamie, 'bye.'

'Bye,' said Jamie. I hung up and went downstairs to turn the television over to something more sensible, but got no farther than the bottom step when the phone went again. I went back up. Just as I did so, a tingle went through me that it might be Eric, but no pips sounded. I grinned and said: 'Yeah? What did you forget?'

'*Forget?* I didn't forget *anything!* I remember everything! *Everything!*' screamed a familiar voice at the other end of the line.

I froze, then gulped, said: 'Er—'

'Why are you accusing me of forgetting things? *What* are you accusing me of forgetting? What? I *haven't* forgotten *anything!*' Eric gasped and spluttered.

'Eric, I'm sorry! I thought you were somebody else!'

'I'm *me!*' he yelled. 'I'm not anybody else! I'm me! *Me!*'

'I thought you were Jamie!' I wailed, closing my eyes.

'*That* dwarf? You bastard!'

'I'm sorry, I—' Then I broke off and thought. 'What do you mean, "that dwarf", in that tone? He's my friend. It isn't his fault he's small,' I told him.

'Oh, yeah?' came the reply. 'How do *you* know?'

'What do you mean how do I know? It wasn't his fault he was born like that!' I said, getting quite angry.

'You only have his word for that.'

'I only have his word for *what?*' I said.

'That he's a dwarf!' Eric spat.

'What?' I shouted, scarcely able to believe my ears. 'I can *see* he's a dwarf, you idiot!'

'That's what he *wants* you to think! Maybe he's really an *alien!* Maybe the rest of them are even smaller than *he* is! How do you know he isn't really a giant alien from a very small race of aliens? Eh?'

'Don't be *stupid!*' I screamed into the phone, gripping it sorely with my burned hand.

'Well, don't say I didn't warn you!' Eric shouted.

'Don't worry!' I shouted back.

'Anyway,' Eric said in a suddenly calm voice, so that for a second or two I thought somebody else had come on the line, and I was left somewhat nonplussed as he went on in level, ordinary speech: 'How are you?'

'Eh?' I said, confused. 'Ah . . . fine. Fine. How are you?'

'Oh, not too bad. Nearly there.'

'What? Here?'

'No. There. Christ, it can't be a bad line over this distance, can it?'

'What distance? Eh? Can it? I don't know.' I put my other hand to my forehead, getting the feeling that I was losing the thread of the conversation entirely.

'I'm nearly *there*,' Eric explained tiredly, with a calm sigh. 'Not nearly *here*. I'm already here. How else could I be calling you from here?'

'But where's "here"?' I said.

'You mean you don't know where you *are* again?' Eric exclaimed incredulously. I closed my eyes again and moaned. He went on; 'And you accuse *me* of forgetting things. Ha!'

'Look, you bloody madman!' I screamed into the green plastic as I gripped it hard and sent spears of pain up my right arm and felt my face contort. 'I'm getting fed up with you calling me up here and being deliberately awkward! *Stop playing games!*' I gasped for breath. 'You know damn well what I mean when I ask where "here " is! I mean where the hell are you! I *know* where I am and you know where I am. Just stop trying to mess me about, *OK*?'

'H'm. Sure, Frank,' Eric said, sounding uninterested. 'Sorry if I was rubbing you up the wrong way.'

'Well—' I started to shout again, then controlled myself and quieted down, breathing hard. 'Well . . . just . . . just don't do that to me. I was only asking where you are.'

'Yeah, that's OK, Frank; I understand,' Eric said evenly. 'But I can't actually tell you where I am or somebody might overhear. Surely you can see that, can't you?'

'All right. All right,' I said. 'But you're not in a call-box, are you?'

'Well, of course I'm not in a call-box,' he said with a bit of an edge in his voice again; then I heard him control his tone. 'Yeah, that's right. I'm in somebody's house. Well, a cottage actually.'

'What?' I said. 'Who? Whose?'

'*I* don't know,' he replied, and I could almost hear him shrug. 'I suppose I could find out if you're really that interested. Are you really that interested?'

'What? No. Yes. I mean, no. What does it matter? But where – I mean how – I mean who do you—?'

'Look, Frank,' Eric said tiredly, 'it's just somebody's little holiday cottage or weekend retreat or something, right? I don't know whose it is; but, as you so perceptively put it, it doesn't matter, all right?'

'You mean you've *broken in* to someobdy's *home*?' I said.

'Yeah; so what? I didn't even have to break in, in fact. I found the key to the back door in the guttering. What's wrong? It's a very nice little place.'

'Aren't you frightened of getting caught?'

'Not much. I'm sitting here in the front room looking down the drive and I can see way down the road. No problem. I've got food and there's a bath and there's a phone and there's a freezer – Christ, you could fit an Alsatian in there – and a bed and everything. Luxury.'

'An *Alsatian*!' I screeched.

'Well, yes, if I had one. I don't, but if I did I could have kept *that* in there. As it is—'

'Don't,' I interrupted, closing my eyes yet again and holding up my hand as though he was there in the house with me. '*Don't* tell me.'

'OK. Well, I just thought I'd ring you and tell you I'm all right, and see how you are.'

'I'm fine. Are you sure you're OK, too?'

'Yeah; never felt better. Feeling great. I think it's my diet; all—'

'Listen!' I broke in desperately, feeling my eyes widen as I thought of what I wanted to ask him. 'You didn't *feel* anything this morning, did you? About dawn? Anything? I mean, anything at all? Nothing inside you – ah – you didn't feel anything? Did you feel anything?'

'What *are* you gibbering about?' Eric said, slightly angrily.

'Did you feel anything this morning, very early?'

'What on earth do you mean – "feel anything"?'

'I mean did you *experience* anything; anything at all about dawn this morning?'

'Well,' Eric said in measured tones, and slowly, 'Funny you should say that. . . .'

'Yes? Yes?' I said excitedly, pressing the receiver so close to my mouth that my teeth clattered off the mouthpiece.

'Not a damn thing. This morning was one of the few I can honestly say I experienced not a thing,' Eric informed me urbanely. 'I was asleep.'

133

'But you said you didn't sleep!' I said furiously.

'Christ, Frank, nobody's perfect.' I could hear him start to laugh.

'But—' I started. I closed my mouth and gritted my teeth. Once more, I closed my eyes.

He said: 'Anyway, Frank, old sport; to be quite honest, this is getting boring. I might call you again but, either way, I'll see you soon. Ta ta.'

Before I could say anything, the line went dead, and I was left fuming and belligerent, holding the telephone and glaring at it like it was to blame. I considered hitting something with it, but decided that would be too much like a bad joke, so I slammed it down on the cradle instead. It chimed once in response and I gave it another glare, then turned my back on it and stamped downstairs, threw myself into an easy chair and punched the buttons on the remote control for the television repeatedly through channel after channel time after time for about ten minutes. At the end of that period I realised that I had got just as much out of watching three programmes simultaneously (the news, yet another awful American crime series and a programme on archaeology) as I ever got from watching the damn things separately. I hurled the control unit away in disgust and stormed outside in the fading light to go and throw a few stones at the waves.

9: What Happened to Eric

I SLEPT fairly late, for me. My father had arrived back at the house just as I returned from the beach, and I had gone to bed at once, so I had a good long sleep. In the morning I called Jamie, got his mother, and found out he had gone to the doctor's but would be straight back. I packed my day-pack and told my father I'd be back in the early evening, then set off for the town.

Jamie was in when I got to his house. We drank a couple of cans of the old Red Death and chatted away; then, after sharing in elevenses and some of his mother's home-made cakes, I left and made my way out of town for the hills behind.

High on a heathered summit, a gentle slope of rock and earth above the Forestry Commission's tree line, I sat on a big rock and ate my lunch. I looked out over the heat-hazed distance, over Porteneil, the pastureland dotted white with sheep, the dunes, the dump, the island (not that you could see it as such;

it looked like part of the land), the sands and the sea. The sky
held a few small clouds; it beat blue over the view, fading to
paleness towards the horizon and the calm expanse of firth and
sea. Larks sung in the air above me and I watched a buzzard
hover as it looked for movement in the grass and heather,
broom and whin beneath. Insects buzzed and danced, and I
waved a fan of fern in front of my face to keep them away as I
ate my sandwiches and drank my orange juice.

To my left, the mounting peaks of the hills marched off
northward, growing gradually higher as they went and fading
into grey and blue, shimmering with distance. I watched the
town beneath me through the binoculars, saw trucks and cars
make their way along the main road, and followed a train as it
headed south, stopping in the town then going on again,
snaking across the level ground before the sea.

I like to get away from the island now and again. Not too
far; I still like to be able to see it if possible, but it is good to
remove oneself sometimes and get a sense of perspective from
a little farther away. Of course, I know how small a piece of
land it is; I'm not a fool. I know the size of the planet and just
how minuscule is that part of it I know. I've watched too much
television and seen too many nature and travel programmes
not to appreciate how limited my own knowledge is in terms of
first-hand experience of other places; but I don't want to go
farther afield, I don't need to travel or see foreign climes or
know different people. I know who I am and I know my
limitations. I restrict my horizons for my own good reasons;
fear – oh, yes, I admit it – and a need for reassurance and safety
in a world which just so happened to treat me very cruelly at an
age before I had any real chance of affecting it.

Also, I have the lesson of Eric.

Eric went away. Eric, with all his brightness, all his
intelligence and sensitivity and promise, left the island and
tried to make his way; chose a path and followed it. That path
led to the destruction of most of what he was, changed him
into a quite different person in whom the similarities to the
sane young man he had been before only appeared obscene.

But he was my brother, and I still loved him in a way. I
loved him despite his alteration the way, I suppose, he had

loved me despite my disability. That feeling of wanting to protect, I suppose, which women are supposed to feel for the young and men are meant to feel for women.

Eric left the island before I was even born, only coming back for holidays, but I think that spiritually he was always there, and when he did return properly, a year after my little accident, when my father thought we both old enough for him to be able to look after the two of us, I didn't resent him being there at all. On the contrary, we got on well from the start, and I'm sure I must have embarrassed him with my slavish following around and copying, though, being Eric, he was too sensitive to other people's feelings to tell me so and risk hurting me.

When he was sent off to private schools I pined; when he came back on holidays I enthused; I jumped and bubbled and got excited. Summer after summer we spent on the island, flying kites, making models from wood and plastic, Lego and Meccano and anything else we found lying about, building dams and constructing huts and trenches. We flew model airplanes, sailed model yachts, built sand-yachts with sails and invented secret societies, codes and languages. He told me stories, inventing them as he went along. We played some stories out: brave soldiers in the dunes and fighting, winning and fighting and fighting and sometimes dying. Those were the only times he deliberately hurt me, when his stories required his own heroic death and I would take it all too seriously as he lay expiring on the grass or the sands, having just blown up the bridge or the dam or the enemy convoy and like as not saved me from death, too; I would choke back tears and punch him lightly as I tried to change the story myself and he refused, slipping away from me and dying; too often dying.

When he had his migraines – sometimes lasting days – I lived on edge, taking cool drinks and some food up to the darkened room on the second floor, creeping in, standing and shaking sometimes if he moaned and shifted on the bed. I was wretched while he suffered, and nothing meant anything; the games and the stories seemed stupid and pointless, and only throwing stones at bottles or seagulls made much sense. I went out fishing for gulls, determined things other than Eric should

137

suffer: when he recovered it was like him coming back for the summer all over again, and I was irrepressible.

Finally, though, that outward urge consumed him, as it does any real man, and it took him away from me, to the outside world with all its fabulous opportunities and awful dangers. Eric decided to follow in his father's footsteps and become a doctor. He told me then that nothing much would change; he would still have most of the summer off, even if he would have to stay down in Glasgow to do hospital work or go around with doctors when they visited people; he told me that we would still be the same when we were together, but I knew it wasn't true, and I could see that in his heart he knew it, too. It was there in his eyes and his words. He was leaving the island, leaving me.

I couldn't blame him, even then, when I felt it hardest. He was Eric, he was my brother, he was doing what he had to do, just like the brave soldier who died for the cause, or for me. How could I doubt or blame him when he had never even started to *suggest* that he doubted or blamed me? My God; all those murders, those three young children killed, one a fratricide. And he simply could not have entertained the idea that I had had a hand in even one of them. I would have known. He couldn't have looked me in the face if he had suspected, he was so incapable of deceit.

So south he went, first one year, carried there earlier than most by his brilliant examination results, then another. The summer in between he came back, but he was changed. He still tried to get along with me the way he always had, but I could feel it was forced. He was away from me, his heart was no longer on the island. It was with the people he knew in the University, with his studies, which he loved; it was in all the rest of the world perhaps, but it was no longer on the island. No longer with me.

We went out, we flew kites, built dams and so on, but it wasn't the same; he was an adult helping me to enjoy myself, not another boy sharing his own joy. It wasn't a bad time, and I was still glad he was there, but he was relieved to go after a month to join some of his student friends on a holiday in the South of France. I mourned what I knew was the passing of the friend and brother I had known, and felt more keenly than at any other time my injury – that thing which I knew would keep me in my adolescent state for ever, would never let me grow up and be a real man, able to make my own way in the world.

I threw that feeling off quickly. I had the Skull, I had the Factory, and I had a vicarious feeling of manly satisfaction in the brilliant performance of Eric on the outside as, for my part, I slowly made myself unchallenged lord of the island and the lands about it. Eric wrote me letters telling me how he was getting on, he called up and spoke to me and my father, and he would make me laugh then on the phone, the way a clever adult can, even though you might not want to let them. He never let me feel that he had totally abandoned me or the island.

Then he had his unfortunate experience which, unknown to me and my father, came on top of other things, and it was enough to kill even the altered person I knew. It was to send Eric flying back and out to something else: an amalgam of both his earlier self (but satanically reversed) and a more worldy-wise man, an adult damaged and dangerous, confused and pathetic and manic all at once. He reminded me of a hologram, shattered; with the whole image contained within one spear-like shard, at once splinter and entirety.

It was during that second year, when he was helping out in a big teaching hospital, that it happened. He didn't even have to be there at the time, down in the guts of the hospital with human rejects; he was helping out in his spare time. Later my father and I heard that Eric had had problems he hadn't told us about. He'd fallen for some girl and it had ended badly, with her telling him she didn't love him after all and going off with somebody else. His migraines had been particularly bad for a while and had interfered with his work. It was because of that as well as the girl that he had been working unofficially in the hospital near the University, helping the nurses on late shifts, sitting in the darkness of the wards with his books while the old and the young and the sick moaned and coughed.

He was doing that the night he had his unpleasant experience. The ward was one where they kept babies and

139

young children so badly deformed they were sure to die outside hospital, and not last much longer even inside. We got a letter explaining most of what had happened from a nurse who had been friendly with my brother, and from the tone of her letter she thought it was wrong to keep some of the children alive; apparently, they were little else than exhibits to be shown to students by the doctors and consultants.

It was a hot, close night in July, and Eric was down in this ghoulish place, near the hospital boiler room and store rooms. He'd had a sore head all day, and while he was in the ward it had worsened into a bad migraine. The ventilation in the place had been faulty for the past couple of weeks, and engineers had been working on the system; that night it was hot and stuffy, and Eric's migraines have always been bad in those conditions. Somebody was coming to replace him in an hour or so, or I suppose even Eric would have admitted defeat and left to go back to his hall of residence and lie down. As it was, he was going round the ward changing nappies and quieting mewling babies and changing dressings and drips or whatever, his head feeling as though it was splitting and his vision distorted with lights and lines.

The child he was attending to when it happened was more or less a vegetable. Amongst its other defects it was totally incontinent, unable to make any other noise apart from a gurgle, couldn't control its muscles properly – even its head had to be supported by a brace – and it wore a metal plate over its head because the bones which should have made up its skull never did grow together, and even the skin over its brain was paper thin.

It had to be fed every few hours with some special mixture, and Eric was doing that when it happened. He had noticed that the child was a little quieter than usual, just sitting there slackly in its chair and staring straight ahead, breathing lightly, eyes glazed and an almost peaceful expression on its usually vacant face. It seemed to be incapable of taking its food, though – one of the few activities that normally it was able to appreciate and even join in. Eric was patient, and held the spoon in front of its unfocused eyes; he put it to its lips where normally the child would have put its tongue out, or try

140

to lean forward and take the spoon into its mouth, but that night it just sat there, not gurgling, not shaking its head or shifting or flapping its arms or rolling its eyes but staring and staring, that curious look on its face which might have been mistaken for happiness.

Eric persevered, sitting closer, trying to ignore the pressing pain in his own head as the migraine got gradually worse. He spoke gently to the child – something that would normally get it to swivel its eyes and shift its head towards the source of the noise, but which that night had no effect at all. Eric checked the sheet of paper by the chair to see if the child had been given any extra medication, but everything appeared normal. He edged closer, crooning, waving the spoon, fighting the waves of pain inside his skull.

Then he saw something, something like a movement, just a tiny little movement, barely visible on the shaved head of the slightly smiling child. Whatever it was was small and slow. Eric blinked, shook his head to try to dislodge the quivering lights of the migraine building inside. He stood up, still holding the spoon with the mushy food on it. He bent closer to the skull of the child, looking closer. He couldn't see anything, but he looked round the edge of the metal skull-cap the child wore, thought he saw something under it, and lifted it easily from the head of the infant to see if there was anything wrong.

A boiler-room worker heard Eric screaming and rushed into the ward brandishing a big spanner; he found Eric crammed into a corner howling as hard as he could at the floor, his head down between his knees as he half-knelt, half-lay, foetal on the tiles. The chair the child was in had been tipped over, and it and the strapped-in child, who was still smiling, lay on the floor a few yards away.

The man from the boiler-room shook Eric but got no response. Then he looked at the child on the chair and went over to it, perhaps to right its chair; he got within a couple of feet, then rushed to the door, throwing up before he got there. A ward sister from the floor above found the man in the corridor still fighting his dry heaves when she came down to see what all the fuss was about. Eric had stopped screaming by that time and gone quiet. The child was still smiling.

The sister righted the child's chair. Whether she choked back any of her own sickness, or felt dizzy, or whether she had seen as bad or worse before and treated it as just something to be coped with, I don't know, but she finally pulled things together, calling for help on the telephone and getting Eric stiffly out of his corner. She put him in a seat, covered the child's head with a towel, and comforted the workman. She had removed the spoon from the open skull of the smiling infant. Eric had stuck it there, perhaps thinking in that first instant of his mania to spoon out what he saw.

Flies had got into the ward, presumably when the air-conditioning had been faulty earlier. They had got underneath the stainless steel of the child's skull-cap and deposited their eggs there. What Eric saw when he lifted that plate up, what he saw with all that weight of human suffering above, with all that mighty spread of closed-in, heat-struck darkened city all around, what he saw with his own skull splitting, was a slowly writhing nest of fat maggots, swimming in their combined digestive juices as they consumed the brain of the child.

In fact, Eric appeared to recover from what happened. He was sedated, he spent a couple of nights in the hospital as a patient, then a few days resting in his room in the residence. He went back to his studies within the week, and attended classes as normal. A few people knew something had happened, and they saw that Eric was quieter, but that was all. My father and I didn't know anything except that he'd been off from his classes for a short while because of a migraine.

Later we heard Eric started drinking a lot, missing classes, turning up at the wrong ones, shouting in his sleep and waking other people on his floor of the residence, taking drugs, missing exams and practical classes. . . . In the end the University had to suggest he took the rest of the year off because he had missed so much work. Eric took it badly; he got all his books and piled them up in the corridor outside his tutor's room and set light to them. He was lucky they didn't prosecute him, but the University authorities took a lenient

142

view of the smoke and the slight damage to their ancient wood panelling, and Eric came back to the island.

But not to me. He refused to have anything to do with me, and kept himself locked in his room, listening to his records very loudly and hardly ever going out except to the town, where he was quickly banned from all four pubs for starting fights and shouting and swearing at people. When he did notice me he would stare at me with his huge eyes, or tap his nose and wink slyly. His eyes had grown dark-set and were underlined by bags, and his nose seemed to twitch a lot, too. Once he picked me up and gave me a kiss on the lips which really made me frightened.

My father grew almost as uncommunicative as Eric. He settled into a morose existence of long walks and dour, introspective silences. He started smoking cigarettes, virtually chain-smoking for a while. For a month or so the house was hell to be in, and I went out a lot, or stayed in my room and watched television.

Then Eric took to frightening small boys from the town, first by throwing worms at them, then by stuffing worms down their shirts as they came back from school. Some of the parents, a teacher and Diggs came to the island to see my father once Eric started trying to force the kids to eat the worms and handfuls of maggots. I sat sweating in my room while they met in the lounge underneath, the parents shouting at my father. Eric was talked to by the doctor, by Diggs, even by a social worker from Inverness, but he didn't say much; he just sat smiling and sometimes mentioned how much protein there was in worms. Once he came back to the house all battered and bleeding, and my father and I assumed some of the bigger boys or a few of the parents had caught him and beaten him.

Apparently dogs had been disappearing from the town for a couple of weeks before some children saw my brother pouring a can of petrol over a little Yorkshire terrier and setting fire to it. Their parents believed them and went looking for Eric, to find him doing the same thing with an old mongrel he had tempted with aniseed balls sweeties, and caught. They chased him through the woods behind the town but lost him.

143

Diggs came to the island again that evening to tell us he had come to arrest Eric for disturbing the peace. He waited until quite late, only accepting a couple of the whiskies my father offered him, but Eric did not return. Diggs left, and my father waited up, but still Eric didn't show. It was three days and five dogs later before he came back, haggard and unwashed and smelling of petrol and smoke, his clothes all torn and his face lean and filthy. My father heard him come in early in the morning, raid the fridge, gulp down several meals at once, and stamp upstairs to bed.

My father crept down to the phone and called Diggs, who arrived before breakfast. Eric must have heard or seen something, though, because he went out through his room window and down the drainpipe to the ground, and made off with Diggs's bike. It was another week and two more dogs before he was finally caught, siphoning petrol from somebody's car in the street. They broke his jaw in the process of making their citizen's arrest, and this time Eric didn't get away.

A few months later he was certified insane. He had had all sorts of tests, tried to escape countless times, assaulted male nurses and social workers and doctors, and threatened all of them with legal action and assassination. He was moved to gradually more and more long-term and secure institutions as his tests and threats and struggles continued. My father and I heard that he quieted down a lot once he settled into the hospital to the south of Glasgow and no longer made his escape attempts, but looking back he was probably just trying – successfully, it would seem – to lull his keepers into a false sense of security.

And now he was making his way back to see us.

I swept my binoculars slowly across the land in front and beneath me, from north to south, from haze to haze, across the town and the roads and the railway and the fields and the sands, and I wondered if under my gaze at any point came the place where Eric was now, if he had got this far already. I felt he was close. I didn't have any good reason, but he had had the time, the call of last night sounded clearer than the others he

144

had made, and . . . I just felt it. He might be here now, lying up waiting for night before he moved, or skulking through the woods or through the whin bushes or within the hollows of the dunes, heading for the house or looking for dogs.

I walked along the ridge of hills, then came down a few miles south of the town, down through the ranks of conifers where distant buzz-saws sounded and the dark masses of the trees were shady and quiet. I went across the railway line and over a few fields of swaying barley, across the road and over the rough sheep-pasture to the sands.

My feet were sore and my legs ached slightly as I walked along the line of hard sand on the beach. A slight wind had come up off the sea, and I was glad of it, because the clouds had all gone and the sun, though sinking gradually, was still powerful. I came to a river I had already crossed once in the hills, and crossed it again near the sea, going up into the dunes a way to where I knew there was a wire bridge. Sheep scattered in front of me, some shorn, some still shaggy, bouncing away with their fractured-sounding baas, then stopping once they thought they were safe and dipping their heads or kneeling to resume cropping the flower-scattered grass.

I remember I used to despise sheep for being so profoundly stupid. I'd seen them eat and eat and eat, I'd watched dogs outsmart whole flocks of them, I'd chased them and laughed at the way they ran, watched them get themselves into all sorts of stupid, tangled situations, and I'd thought they quite deserved to end up as mutton, and that being used as wool-making machines was too good for them. It was years, and a long slow process, before I eventually realised just what sheep really represented: not their own stupidity, but our power, our avarice and egotism.

After I'd come to understand evolution and know a little about history and farming, I saw that the thick white animals I laughed at for following each other around and getting caught in bushes were the product of generations of farmers as much as generations of sheep; *we* made them, we moulded them from the wild, smart survivors that were their ancestors so that they would become docile, frightened, stupid, tasty wool-producers. We didn't want them to be smart, and to some

145

extent their aggression and their intelligence went together. Of course, the rams are brighter, but even they are demeaned by the idiotic females they have to associate with and inseminate.

The same principle applies to chickens and cows and almost anything we've been able to get our greedy, hungry hands on for long enough. It occasionally occurs to me that something the same might have happened to women but, attractive though the theory might be, I suspect I'm wrong.

Home in time for dinner, I wolfed down my eggs, steak, chips and beans, and spent the rest of the evening watching television and picking bits of dead cow out of my mouth with a match.

10: Running Dog

IT ALWAYS annoyed me that Eric went crazy. Although it wasn't an on–off thing, sane one minute, mad the next, I don't think there is much doubt that the incident with the smiling child triggered something in Eric that led, almost inevitably, to his fall. Something in him could not accept what had happened, could not fit in what he had seen with the way he thought things ought to be. Maybe some deep part of him, buried under layers of time and growth like the Roman remains of a modern city, still believed in God, and could not suffer the realisation that, if such an unlikely being did exist, it could suffer that to happen to any of the creatures it had supposedly fashioned in its own image.

Whatever it was that disintegrated in Eric then, it was a weakness, a fundamental flaw that a real man should not have had. Women, I know from watching hundreds – maybe thousands – of films and television programmes, cannot withstand really major things happening to them; they get raped, or their loved one dies, and they go to pieces, go crazy and commit suicide, or just pine away until they die. Of course, I realise that not all of them will react that way, but obviously it's the rule, and the ones who don't obey it are in the minority.

There must be a few strong women, women with more man in their character than most, and I suspect that Eric was the victim of a self with just a little too much of the woman in it. That sensitivity, that desire not to hurt people, that delicate, mindful brilliance – these things were his partly because he thought too much like a woman. Up until his nasty experience it never really bothered him, but just at that moment, in that extremity of circumstance, it was enough to break him.

I blame my father, not to mention whatever stupid bitch it was threw him over for another man. My father must take the blame in part at least because of that nonsense in Eric's early years, letting him dress as he wanted and giving him the choice of dresses and trousers; Harmsworth and Morag Stove were quite right to be worried about the way their nephew was being brought up, and did the proper thing in offering to look after him. Everything might have been different if my father hadn't had those daft ideas, if my mother hadn't resented Eric, if the Stoves had taken him away earlier; but it happened the way it did, and as such I hope my father blames himself as much as I blame him. I want him to feel the weight of that guilt upon him all the time, and have sleepless nights because of it, and bad dreams that wake him up in a sweat on cool nights once he does get to sleep. He deserves it.

Eric didn't ring that night after my walk in the hills. I went to bed fairly early, but I know I'd have heard the phone if it had gone, and I slept without a break, tired after my long trek. The next day I was up at the normal time, went out for a walk along the sands in the coolness of the morning, and came back in time for a good big cooked breakfast.

I felt restless, my father was quieter than usual, and the heat built quickly, making the house very stuffy even with the windows open. I wandered about the rooms, looking out through those opened spaces, leaning on ledges, scouring the land with closed-up eyes. Eventually, with my father dozing in a deckchair, I went to my own room, changed to a T-shirt and my light waistcoat with the pockets, filled them up with useful things, slung my day-pack over one shoulder and set off to have a good look round the approaches to the island, and maybe take in the dump, too, if there weren't too many flies.

I put my sunglasses on, and the brown Polaroids made the colours more vivid. I started to sweat as soon as I stepped out of the door. A warm breeze, hardly cooling at all, swirled uncertainly from a few directions, brought smells of grass and flowers. I walked steadily, up the path, over the bridge, down the mainland line of the creek and the stream, following the course of the burn and jumping its small offshoots and tributaries down to the dam-building area. I turned north then, going up the line of the sea-facing dunes, taking them by their sandy summits despite the heat and the exertion of climbing their southern faces, so that I could gain the benefit of the views they offered.

Everything shimmered in that heat, became uncertain and shifting. The sand was hot when I touched it, and insects of all sorts and sizes buzzed and whirred about me. I waved them away.

Now and again I used the binoculars, wiping the sweat from my brows and lifting the glasses to my eyes, inspecting the distance through the heat-thick quivering air. My scalp crawled with perspiration, and my crotch itched. I checked the things I had brought with me more often than I usually did, absently weighing the small cloth bag of steelies, touching the Bowie knife and catapult on my belt, making sure I still had my lighter, wallet, comb, mirror, pen and paper. I drank from the small flask of water that I had, though it was warm and tasted stale already.

I could see some interesting-looking pieces of flotsam and jetsam when I looked over the sands and the lapping sea, but I stayed on the dunes, taking the higher ones when I had to, going far north, over streams and through small marshes, past the Bomb Circle and the place I had never really named, where Esmerelda took off.

I only thought of them after I had passed them.

After an hour or so I turned inland, then south, along the last of the mainland dunes, looking out over the scrubby pasture where the sheep moved slow, like maggots, over the land, eating. Once I stood a while and watched a great bird, high up against the unbroken blue, wheeling and spiralling on the thermals, turning this way and that. Below it a few gulls shifted, their wings outstretched and their white necks pointing about as they searched for something. I found a dead frog high on a dune, dried and bloody on its back and stuck with sand, and wondered how it had got up there. Probably dropped by a bird.

I put on my little green cap eventually, shielding my eyes from the glare. I swung down over the path, level with the island and the house. I kept going, still stopping now and again to use the binoculars. Cars and trucks glinted through the trees, a mile or so away on the road. A helicopter flew over once, most likely heading for one of the rig yards or a pipeline.

I reached the dump just after noon, coming through some small trees to it. I sat down in the shade of one tree and inspected the place with the glasses. Some gulls were there, but no people. A little smoke drifted up from a fire near its centre, and spread around it was all the debris from the town and its area: cardboard and black plastic bags and the gleaming, battered whiteness of old washing machines, cookers and fridges. Papers picked themselves up and went round in a circle for a minute or so as a tiny whirlwind started, then dropped again.

I picked my way through the dump, savouring its rotten, slightly sweet smell. I kicked at some of the rubbish, turned a few interesting things over with one booted foot, but could see nothing worthwhile. One of the things I had come to like about the dump over the years was the way that it never stayed the same; it moved like something huge and alive, spreading like an immense amoeba as it absorbed the healthy land and the collective waste. But this day it looked tired and boring. I felt impatient with it, almost angry. I threw a couple of aerosol cans into the weak fire burning in the middle, but even they provided little diversion, popping effetely inside the pale flames. I left the dump and headed south again.

150

Near a small stream about a kilometre from the dump there was a large bungalow, a holiday home looking out over the sea. It was closed up and deserted, and there were no fresh tracks on the bumpy trail leading down to it and past it to the beach. It was down that track that Willie, one of Jamie's other friends, had driven us in his old Mini van to race along the sands and skid about.

I looked through the windows at the empty rooms, the old unmatching furniture sitting in the shadows looking dusty and neglected. An old magazine lay on a table, one corner yellowed with sunlight. In the shade of the gable end of the house I sat down and finished my water, took off my cap and wiped my forehead with my handkerchief. In the distance I could hear muffled explosions from the range farther down the coast, and once a jet came tearing in over the calm sea, heading due west.

Away from the house a ridge of low hills started, topped with whin and stunted trees shaped by the wind. I trained the binoculars on them, waving flies away, my head starting to ache just a little and my tongue dry despite the warm water I had just drunk. When I lowered the glasses and put the Polaroids back down I heard it.

Something howled. Some animal – my God, I hoped it wasn't a human making that noise – screamed in torment. It was a rising, anguished wail, the note produced only by an animal *in extremis*, the noise you hope no living thing ever has to make.

I sat with the sweat dripping off me, parched and aching with the baking heat; but I shivered. I shook with a wave of cold like a dog shaking itself dry, from one end to the other. The hair on the back of my neck unstuck itself from the sweat, stood. I got up quickly, hands scrabbling on the warm wood of the house wall, binoculars bumping on my chest. The scream came from the ridge. I pushed the Polaroids back up, used the glasses again, bashing them on the bones above my eyes as I fought with the focusing-wheel. My hands shook.

A black shape shot out of the whins, trailing smoke. It raced down the slope over the yellow-spangled grass, under a fence. My hands bounced the view around as I tried to pan the binoculars to follow it. The keen wail sounded over the air, thin and terrible. I lost the thing behind some bushes, then saw it again, burning as it ran and jumped over grass and reed, raising spray. My mouth dried completely; I couldn't swallow, I was choking, but I tracked the animal as it skidded and turned, yelping high, bounding into the air, falling, seeming to leap on the spot. Then it disappeared, a few hundred metres from me and about as much down from the ridge of the hill.

I swept the glasses quickly back up to look at the top of the ridge again, scanned along it, back, down, back up, along again, stopped to stare intently at a bush, shook my head, scanned the length again. Some irrelevant part of my brain thought about how in films, when people look through binoculars and you see what they are supposed to be seeing, it's always a sort of figure-of-eight on its side that you see, but whenever I look through them I see more or less a perfect circle. I brought the glasses down, looked about quickly, saw nobody, then I sprinted out of the shadow of the house, leaped the small wire fence that marked the garden, and ran towards the ridge.

On the ridge I stood for a moment, head down to my knees, gasping for breath, letting the perspiration drip off my hair and on to the bright grass at my feet. My T-shirt stuck to me. I put my hands on my knees and lifted my head, straining my eyes to look along the line of whin and trees on the ridge's top. I looked down the far side and over the fields beyond to the next line of whin, which marked the cutting the railway line ran through. I jogged along the ridge, head sweeping to and fro, until I found a little patch of burning grass. I stamped it out, looked for tracks and found them. I ran faster, despite my protesting throat and lungs, found some more burning grass and a whin bush just catching. I beat them out, went on.

Down in a small hollow on the land side of the ridge some trees had grown almost normally, only their tops, sticking out over the lee of the line of small hills, leaned out from the sea, twisted by the wind. I ran into the grassy hollow, into the moving pattern of shade provided by the slowly swaying

152

leaves and branches. There was a circle of stones around a blackened centre. I looked around, saw a piece of flattened grass. I stopped, calmed myself, looked around again, at the trees and the grass and the ferns, but could see nothing else. I went to the stones, felt them and the ashes in their circle. They were hot, too hot to keep my hands on them, though they were in shade. I could smell petrol.

I climbed out of the hollow and up a tree, steadied myself and slowly inspected the whole area, using my binoculars when I had to. Nothing.

I climbed down, stood for a second, then took a deep breath and ran down the sea-facing side of the hills, heading across diagonally to where I knew the animal had been. I changed course once, to beat out another small fire. I surprised a cropping sheep; jumped right over it as it startled and bounced away, baaing.

The dog lay in the stream leading out of the marsh. It was still alive, but most of its black coat was gone, and the skin underneath was livid and seeping. It quivered in the water, making me shiver, too. I stood on the bank and looked at it. It could only see with one unburned eye as it raised its shaking head out of the water. In the little pool around it floated bits of clotted, half-burned fur. I caught a hint of the smell of burned meat, and felt a weight settle in my neck, just below my Adam's apple.

I took out my bag of steelies, brought one to the sling of the catapult as I unhooked it from my belt, stretched my arms out, one hand by my face, where it was wetted by sweat, then released.

The dog's head jerked out of the water, splashing down then up, sending the animal away from me, and over on one side. It floated downstream a little, then bumped, caught by the bank. Some blood flowed from the hole where that one eye had been. 'Frank'll get you,' I whispered.

I dragged the dog out and dug a hole in the peaty ground upstream with my knife, gagging now and again on the smell of the corpse. I buried the animal, looked round again, then, after judging the slightly stiffened breeze, walked away a bit

153

and set fire to the grass. The blaze swept over the last bits of the dog's fiery trail, and over its grave. It stopped at the stream, where I had thought it would, and I stamped out a few patches of stray fire on the far bank, where a couple of embers had blown.

When it was over, and the dog buried, I turned for home and ran.

I got back to the house without incident, downed two pints of water, and tried to relax in a cool bath with a carton of orange juice balanced on the side. I was still shaking, and spent a time washing the smell of burning out of my hair. Vegetarian cooking smells came up from the kitchen, where my father was preparing a meal.

I was sure I had almost seen my brother. That wasn't where he was camped, I decided, but he had been there, and I had just missed him. In a way I was relieved, and that was difficult to accept, but it was the truth.

I sank back, let the water wash over me.

I came down to the kitchen with my dressing-gown on. My father was sitting at the table with a vest and shorts on, elbows on the table, staring at the *Inverness Courier*. I put the carton of orange juice back in the fridge and lifted the lid of the pot where a curry was cooling. Bowls of salad to accompany it lay on the table. My father turned the pages of the paper, ignoring me.

'Hot, isn't it?' I said, for want of anything else.

'Hnnh.'

I sat down at the other end of the table. My father turned another page, head down. I cleared my throat.

'There was a fire, down by the new house. I saw it. I went and put it out,' I said, to cover myself.

'It's the weather for it,' my father said, without looking up. I nodded to myself, scratching my crotch quietly through the towelling of the dressing-gown.

'I saw from the forecast it's supposed to break tomorrow late sometime.' I shrugged. 'So they said.'

'Well, we'll see,' my father said, turning the paper back to the front page as he got up to have a look at the curry. I nodded to myself again, toying with the end of the belt of the dressing-gown, looking casually at the paper. My father bent to sniff the mixture in the pot. I stared.

I looked at him, got up, went round to the chair he had been sitting in, stood as though I was looking out of the door, but in fact with my eyes slanted towards the paper. MYSTERY BLAZE IN HOLIDAY COTTAGE, said the bottom eighth of the front page on the left-hand side. A holiday home just south of Inverness had gone up in flames shortly before the paper went to press. The police were still investigating.

I went back to the other end of the table, sat down.

We eventually had the curry and the salad, and I started sweating again. I used to think that I was weird because I found that the morning after I had eaten a curry my armpits smelled of the stuff, but I have since found that Jamie has experienced the same effect, so I don't feel so bad. I ate the curry and had a banana and some yoghurt along with it, but it was still too hot, and my father, who has always had a rather masochistic approach to the dish, left almost half of his.

I was still in my dressing-gown, sitting watching the television in the lounge, when the phone went. I started for the door, but heard my father go from his study to answer it, so I stayed by the door to listen. I couldn't hear much, but then footsteps came down the stairs and I ran back to my chair, flopped into it and put my head over on one side, eyes closed and mouth open. My father opened the door.

'Frank. It's for you.'

'H'm?' I said slowly, opening my eyes gummily, looking at the television, then getting up a little unsteadily. My father left the door open for me and retreated to his study. I went to the phone.

'M'm? Hello?'

''allah-oh, zet Frenk?' said a very English voice.

'Yes, hello?' I said, puzzled.

'Heh-heh, Frankie boy!' Eric shouted. 'Well, here I am, in your thorax of the woods and still eating the old *hot dogs*! Ho ho! So how are ye, me young bucko? Stars going OK for you, are they? What sign are you, anyway? I forget.'

'Canis.'

'Woof! Really?'

'Yeah. What sign are you?' I asked, dutifully following one of Eric's old routines.

'Cancer!' came the screamed reply.

'Benign or malignant?' I said tiredly.

'Malignant!' Eric screeched. 'I've got *crabs* at the moment!'

I took my ear away from the plastic while Eric guffawed. 'Listen, Eric —' I began.

'How're ye doin'? How's things? Howzithingin'? Are you well? Howzitgon? Andyerself? Wotchermait. Like where's your head at this moment in time? Where are you comin' from? Christ, Frank, do you know why Volvos *whistle*? Well, neither do I, but who cares? What did Trotsky say? "I need Stalin like I need a hole in the head." Ha ha ha ha ha! Actually I don't like these German cars; their headlights are too close together. Are ye well, Frankie?'

'Eric—'

'To bed, to sleep; perchance to masturbate. Ah, there's the rub! Ho ho ho!'

'Eric,' I said, looking round and up the stairs to make sure my father was nowhere in evidence. 'Will you shut *up*!'

'What?' Eric said, in a small, hurt voice.

'The *dog*,' I hissed. 'I saw that dog today. The one down by the new house. I was there. I saw it.'

'What dog?' Eric said, sounding perplexed. I could hear him sigh heavily, and something clattered in the background.

'Don't try to mess me around, Eric; I saw it. I want you to stop, understand? No more dogs. Can you hear me? Do you get it? *Well*?'

'What? What dogs?'

'You heard. You're too close. No more dogs. Leave them alone. And no kids, either. No worms. Just forget about it. Come and see us if you want to – that'd be nice – but no worms, no burning dogs. I'm serious, Eric. You'd better believe it.'

'Believe what? What are you talking about?' he said in a plaintive voice.

'You heard,' I said, and put the phone down. I stood by the

156

telephone, looking upstairs. In a few seconds it rang again. I picked it up, heard pips go, and replaced it on the cradle. I stayed there for a few more minutes, but nothing else happened.

As I started to go back to the lounge my father came along from the study, wiping his hands on a cloth, followed by odd smells, his eyes wide.

'Who was that?'

'Just Jamie,' I said, 'putting on a funny voice.'

'Hnnh,' he said, apparently relieved, and went back.

Apart from his curry repeating on him my father was very quiet. When the evening started to cool I went out, just once round the island. Clouds were coming in off the sea, closing the sky like a door and trapping the day's heat over the island. Thunder rumbled on the other side of the hills, without light. I slept fitfully, lying sweating and tossing and turning on my bed, until a bloodshot dawn rose over the sands of the island.

11: The Prodigal

I WOKE from my last bout of restless sleep with the duvet on the floor beside the bed. Nevertheless, I was sweating. I got up, had a shower, shaved carefully, and climbed into the loft before the heat up there got too severe.

In the loft it was very stuffy. I opened the skylights and stuck my head out, surveying the land behind and the sea in front with my binoculars. It was still overcast; the light seemed tired and the breeze tasted stale. I tinkered with the Factory a bit, feeding the ants and the spider and the Venus, checking wires, dusting the glass over the face, testing batteries and oiling doors and other mechanisms, all more to reassure myself than anything else. I dusted the altar as well as arranged everything on it carefully, using a ruler to make sure all the little jars and other pieces were arranged perfectly symmetrically on it.

I was sweating again by the time I came down, but couldn't be bothered having another shower. My father was up, and made breakfast while I watched some Saturday-morning television. We ate in silence. I took a tour round the island in the morning, going to the Bunker and getting the Head Bag so I could do any necessary repair work to the Poles as I made my way round.

It took me longer than usual to complete the circuit because I kept stopping and going to the top of the nearest tall dune to look out over the approaches. I never did see anything. The heads on the Sacrifice Poles were in fairly good repair. I had to replace a couple of mice heads, but that was about all. The other heads and the streamers were intact. I found a dead gull lying on the mainland face of a dune, opposite the island's centre. I took the head and buried the rest near a Pole. I put the head, which was starting to smell, in a plastic bag and stuffed it in the Head Bag with the dried ones.

I heard then saw the birds go up as somebody came along the path, but I knew it was only Mrs Clamp. I climbed a dune to watch, and saw her pedalling over the bridge with her ancient delivery-bike. I took another look over the pastureland and dunes beyond, once she had disappeared round the dune before the house, but there was nothing, just sheep and gulls. Smoke came from the dump, and I could just hear the steady grumble of an old diesel on the railway line. The sky stayed overcast but bright, and the wind sticky and uncertain. Out to sea I could make out golden slivers near the horizon where the water glittered under breaks in the cloud, but they were far, far out.

I completed my round of the Sacrifice Poles, then spent half an hour near the old winch indulging in a bit of target practice. I set up a few cans on the rusty iron of the drum housing, went back thirty metres and brought them all down with my catapult, using only three extra steelies for the six cans. I set them up again once I had recovered all but one of the big ball-bearings, went back to the same position and threw pebbles at the cans, this time taking fourteen shots before all the cans were down. I ended up throwing the knife at a tree by the old sheep-pen a few times and was pleased to find I was judging the number of tumbles well, the blade whacking into the much-cut bark straight each time.

Back in the house I washed, changed my shirt and then appeared in the kitchen in time for Mrs Clamp serving up the first course, which for some reason was piping-hot broth. I waved a slice of soft, smelly white bread over it while Mrs Clamp bent to the bowl and slurped noisily and my father crumbled wholemeal bread, which appeared to have wood shavings in it, over his plate.

'And how are you, Mrs Clamp?' I asked pleasantly.

'Oh, *I'm* all right,' Mrs Clamp said, drawing her brows together like a snagged end of wool being unravelled from a sock. She completed the frown and directed it at the dripping spoon just under her chin, telling it: 'Oh, yes, *I'm* all right.'

'Isn't it hot?' I said, and hummed. I went on flapping the bread over my soup while my father looked at me darkly.

'It's summer,' Mrs Clamp explained.

'Oh, yes,' I said. 'I'd forgotten.'

'Frank,' my father said rather unclearly, his mouth full of vegetables and wood shavings, 'I don't suppose you recall the capacity of these spoons, do you?'

'A quarter-gill?' I suggested innocently. He glowered and sipped some more soup. I kept on flapping, stopping only to disturb the brown skin that was forming over the surface of my broth. Mrs Clamp sipped again.

'And how are things in the town, Mrs Clamp?' I asked.

'Very well, as far as *I* know,' Mrs Clamp informed her soup. I nodded. My father was blowing at his spoon. 'The Mackies' *dog* has gone missing, or so *I* was told,' Mrs Clamp added. I raised my brows slightly and smiled in a concerned way. My father stopped and stared, and the noise of his soup dribbling off his spoon – the end of which had started to drop slightly just after Mrs Clamp's sentence – echoed round the room like piss going into a toilet bowl.

'Really?' I said, keeping on flapping. 'What a shame. Just as well my brother's not around or he'd be getting the blame of it.' I smiled, glanced at my father, then back at Mrs Clamp, who was watching me with narrowed eyes through the rising steam from her soup. Dough fatigue set into the piece of bread I was using to fan the soup, and it fell apart. I caught the falling end smartly with my free hand and returned it to my side plate, raising my spoon and taking a tentative sip from the surface of the broth.

'H'm,' Mrs Clamp said.

'Mrs Clamp couldn't get your beefburgers today,' my father said, clearing his throat on the first syllable of 'couldn't', 'so she got you mince instead.'

'Unions!' Mrs Clamp muttered darkly, spitting into her soup. I put one elbow on the table, rested my cheek on a fist and looked puzzledly at her. To no avail. She didn't look up, and eventually I shrugged to myself and carried on sipping. My father had put his spoon down, wiping his brow with one sleeve and using a fingernail in an attempt to remove a piece of what I assumed to be wood shaving from between two upper teeth.

'There was a wee fire down by the new house yesterday, Mrs Clamp; I put it out, you know. I was down there and I saw it and I put it out,' I said.

'Don't boast, boy,' my father said. Mrs Clamp held her tongue.

'Well, I did,' I smiled.

'I'm sure Mrs Clamp isn't interested.'

'Oh, *I* wouldn't say that,' Mrs Clamp said, nodding her head in slightly confusing emphasis.

'There, you see?' I said, humming as I looked at my father and nodded towards Mrs Clamp, who slurped noisily.

I kept quiet through the main course, which was a stew, and only noted during the rhubarb and custard that it had a novel addition to the medley of flavours, when in fact the milk it had been made from had obviously been most profoundly off. I smiled, my father growled and Mrs Clamp slurped her custard and spat her stumps of rhubarb out on to her napkin. To be fair, it was a little undercooked.

Dinner cheered me up immensely and, although the afternoon was hotter than the morning, I felt more energetic. There were no slits of distant brightness out over the sea, and there was a thickness about the light coming through the clouds that went with the charge in the air and the slack wind. I went out, going once round the island at a brisk jog; I watched Mrs Clamp depart for the town, then I walked out in the same direction to sit on top of a tall dune a few hundred metres into the mainland and sweep the sweltering land with my binoculars.

Sweat rolled off me as soon as I stopped moving, and I could feel a slight ache start in my head. I had taken a little water with me, so I drank it, then refilled the can from the nearest stream. My father was doubtless right that sheep shat in the streams, but I was sure I had long since grown immune to anything I could catch from the local burns, having drunk from them for years while I had been damming them. I drank more water than I really felt like and returned to the top of the dune. In the distance the sheep were still, lying on the grass. Even the gulls were absent, and only the flies were still active. The smoke from the dump still drifted, and another line of hazy blue rose from the plantations in the hills, coming up from the edge of a clearing where they were harvesting the trees for the pulp mill farther up the shore of the firth. I strained to hear the sound of the saws, but couldn't.

I was scanning the binoculars over that view to the south when I saw my father. I went over him, then jerked back. He disappeared, then reappeared. He was on the path, heading for the town. I was looking over to where the Jump was, and saw him climb the side of the dune I liked to power the bike down; I had first caught sight of him as he had crested the Jump itself. As I watched, he seemed to stumble on the path just before the summit of the hill, but recovered and kept going. His cap vanished over the far side of the dune. I thought he looked unsteady, as though he was drunk.

I put the glasses down and rubbed my slightly scratchy chin. This was unusual, too. He hadn't said anything about going into the town. I wondered what he was up to.

I ran down the dune, leaped the stream and went back to the house at a fast cruise. I could smell whisky when I went through the back door. I thought back to how long ago we had eaten and Mrs Clamp had left. About an hour, an hour and a half. I went into the kitchen, where the smell of whisky was stronger, and there on the table lay an empty half-bottle of

162

malt, one glass on its side nearby. I looked in the sink for another glass, but there were only dirty dishes lying in it. I frowned.

It was unlike my father to leave things unwashed. I picked up the whisky-bottle and looked for a black biro mark on the label, but there was nothing. That might mean it had been a fresh bottle. I shook my head to myself, wiped my forehead with a dishcloth. I took off my pocketed waistcoat and laid it over a chair.

I went out into the hall. As soon as I looked upstairs I saw that the phone was off the hook, lying by the side of the set. I went up to it quickly, picked it up. It was making an odd noise. I replaced it on the cradle, waited a few seconds, picked it up again and got the usual dialling tone. I threw it down and sprinted upstairs to the study, twisting the handle and throwing my weight against it. It was solid.

'Shit!' I said. I could guess what had happened and I had hoped my father might have left the study unlocked. Eric must have called. Dad gets the call, is shocked, gets drunk. Probably heading for the town to get more drink. Gone to the off-licence, or – I glanced at my watch – was this the weekend the Rob Roy's all-day licence started? I shook my head; it didn't matter. Eric must have called. My father was drunk. He was probably going to town to get more drunk, or to see Diggs. Or maybe Eric had arranged a rendezvous. No, that wasn't likely; surely he would contact me first.

I ran upstairs, went up into the close heat of the loft, opened the land-side skylight again and surveyed the approaches through the glasses. I came back down, locked the house and went back out, jogging to the bridge and up the path, making detours for all the tall dunes once more. Everything looked normal. I stopped at the place I had last seen my father, just on the crest of the hill leading down to the Jump. I scratched my crotch in exasperation, wondering what was the best thing to do. I didn't feel right about leaving the island, but I had a suspicion that it was in or near the town that things might start happening. I thought of calling Jamie up, but he probably wasn't in the best condition to go traipsing round Porteneil looking for Father or keeping his nostrils open for the smell of burning dog.

I sat down on the path and tried to think. What would Eric's next move be? He might wait for night to approach (I was sure he would approach; he wouldn't come all this way just to turn away at the last moment, would he?), or he might have risked enough already in telephoning and consider he had little left to lose by heading for the house right away. But of course he might as well have done that yesterday, so what was keeping him? He was planning something. Or maybe I had been too abrupt with him on the phone. Why had I hung up on him? Idiot! Perhaps he was going to give himself up, or turn tail! All because I had rejected him, his own brother!

I shook my head angrily and stood up. None of this was getting me anywhere. I had to assume that Eric was going to get in touch. That meant that I had to go back to the house, where either he would phone me or he would arrive sooner or later. Besides, it was the centre of my power and strength, and also the place I had the most need to protect. Thus resolved, heart lightened now that I had a definite plan – even if it was more a plan of inaction than anything else – I turned for the house and jogged back.

The house had grown still more stuffy while I had been away. I plonked myself down in a chair in the kitchen, then got up to wash the glass and dispose of the whisky-bottle. I had a long drink of orange juice, then filled a pitcher full of juice and ice, took a couple of apples, half a loaf of bread and some cheese and transported the lot up into the attic. I got the chair which normally sits in the Factory and propped it up on a platform of ancient encyclopedias, swung the skylight facing the mainland right back, and made a cushion from some old, faded curtains. I settled into my little throne and started watching through the binoculars. After a while I fished out the old bakelite-and-valves radio from the back of a box of toys and plugged it into the second light fixture with an adaptor. I turned on Radio Three, which was playing a Wagner opera; just the thing to put me in the mood, I thought. I went back to the skylight.

Holes had broken in the cloud-cover in a few places; they moved slowly, putting patches of land into a brassy, glaring sunlight. Sometimes the light shone on the house; I watched the shadow of my shed move slowly round as the late afternoon became early evening and the sun moved round above the frayed clouds. A slow pattern of reflecting windows glinted from the new housing estate in the trees, slightly above the old part of the town. Gradually one set of windows stopped reflecting, gradually others took their place, all punctuated by occasional stabs as windows were shut or opened, or cars moved in the council streets. I drank some of the juice, held ice cubes in my mouth, while the hot breath of the house wafted out around me. I kept the binoculars on their steady sweepings, scanning as far to the north and south as I could without falling out of the skylight. The opera ended, was replaced by some awful modern music for what sounded like Heretic-on-a-rack and Burning Dog, which I let play because it was stopping me from getting sleepy.

Just after half-past six, the phone rang. I leaped out of the chair, dived down the door out of the loft and skidded down the stairs, flicking the phone off the cradle and up to my mouth in one clean movement. I felt a buzz of excitement at how well co-ordinated I was today, and said, quite calmly: 'Yes?'

'Frang?' my father's voice said, slow and slurred. 'Frang, iss 'at you?'

I let the contempt I felt creep into my voice: 'Yes, Dad, it's me. What is it?'

' 'M in the town, son,' he said quietly, as though he was about to start crying. I heard him take a deep breath. 'Frang, you know 've always loved you . . . 'm . . . 'm callin' . . . callin' from the town, son. Want you to come here, son, want you to come . . . come here. They've caught Eric, son.'

I froze. I stared at the wallpaper above the little table in the corner of the turn of the stairs where the phone sat. The wallpaper was a leafy pattern, green on white, with a sort of trellis-work peeping through the greenery in places. It was slightly squint. I hadn't really noticed that wallpaper for years, certainly not in all the years I had been answering the phone. It was horrible. My father was a fool to have chosen it.

'Frang?' He cleared his throat. 'Frank, son?' he said, almost clearly, then relapsed: 'Frang, ari therr? Say somin, son.

165

'S me. Say somin, son. Ah said they caugh' Eric. Ji hear, son? Frang, istill therr?'

'I—' My dry mouth tripped me, and the sentence died. I cleared my throat carefully, began again. 'I heard you, Dad. They've caught Eric. I heard. I'll be right in. Where'll I meet you, at the police station?'

'Naw, naw, son. Naw, mee' me ou'side the . . . ou'side the . . . lib'ary. Yeah, the lib'ary. Mee' me therr.'

'The *library*?' I said. 'Why there?'

'Righ', see y', son. Mon hurry up, eh?' I heard him clatter the receiver for a few seconds, then the line went quiet. I put the phone down slowly, feeling a sharpness in my lungs, a steely sensation that went with the thudding of my heart and my lightened head.

I stood for a while, then went back up the stairs to the loft to close the skylight and turn the radio off. My legs were a little sore and tired, I realised; perhaps I had been overdoing things a bit recently.

The breaks in the cloud overhead were moving slowly inland as I walked back up the path towards the town. It was dark for half-seven, a summery gloom of soft light everywhere over the dry land. A few birds stirred themselves lethargically as I went past. Quite a few were perching on the wires of the telephone line snaking its way to the island on skinny poles. Sheep made their ugly, broken noises, little lambs bleated back. Birds sat on barbed-wire fences farther on, where the snagged tufts of dirty wool showed the sheep trails underneath. Despite all the water I had drunk during the day, my head was starting to ache dully again. I sighed and kept on walking, through the slowly diminishing dunes and past the rough fields and straggly pastureland.

I sat down, back against sand, just before I left the dunes entirely, and wiped my brow. I flicked a little sweat from my fingers, looked out over the static sheep and the perched birds. In the town I could hear bells, probably from the Catholic chapel. Or maybe the word had spread their bloody dogs were safe. I sneered, snorted through my nose in a sort of half-laugh, and looked over the grass and scrub and weed to the steeple of the Church of Scotland. I could almost see the library from here. I felt my feet complain, and knew that I shouldn't have sat down. They'd be sore when I started walking again. I knew damn well that I was just delaying getting to the town, just as I had delayed leaving the house after my father had telephoned. I looked back at the birds, strung like notes along the same wires which had brought the news. They were avoiding one section, I noticed.

I frowned, looked closer, frowned again. I felt for my binoculars, but I touched my own chest; I had left them back at the house. I got up and started walking across the rough ground, away from the path, then I jogged; then I ran, finally sprinting across the weeds and rushes, vaulting a fence on to the pasture where the sheep rose and scattered, cackling plaintively.

I was breathless by the time I got to the telephone line.

And it was down. The freshly cut wire hung against the wood of the land-side pole. I looked up, made sure I wasn't seeing things. A few of the birds nearby had flown off, and they circled, calling in their dark voices through the almost still air over the parched grass. I ran down to the island-side pole on the other side of the break. An ear, covered in short white and black fur, and still bleeding, was nailed to the wood. I touched it and I smiled. I looked round wildly, then calmed myself again. I set my face to the town where the steeple pointed like a finger, accusatory.

'You lying bastard,' I breathed, then took off for the island again, gathering pace as I went, hitting the path and letting rip, pounding down its beaten surface, careering down to the Jump and sailing over it. I shouted and whooped, then I shut up, and kept my precious breath for running.

I got back to the house, yet again, and raced up lathered in sweat to the loft, stopping briefly at the telephone to check it. Sure enough, it was quite dead. I ran on upstairs, back to the loft and the skylight, took a quick look round with the glasses, then got myself together, arming and checking. I settled back into the chair, switched the radio back on, and kept looking.

He was out there somewhere. Thank God for the birds. My

167

stomach thrilled, sending a wave of gut-joy through me, making me shiver despite the heat. That lying old shit, trying to lure me away from the house just because *he* was too frightened to face Eric. My God, I had been stupid not to hear the sheer mendacity in his sodden voice. And he had the nerve to shout at me for drinking. At least I did it when I knew I could afford to, not when I knew I'd need all my faculties at their peak to deal with a crisis. The shit. Call himself a man!

I had a few more drinks from the still cool jug of orange, ate an apple and some bread and cheese, went on scanning. The evening darkened quickly as the sun dipped and the cloud closed up. The thermals which had opened the holes over the land were dying, and the blanket hanging over the hills and the plain reasserted itself, grey and featureless. After a while I heard thunder again, and something in the air turned sharp and threatening. I was keyed up, and couldn't help waiting for the phone to ring, though I knew that it wouldn't. How long would it take for my father to realise I was late? Had he expected me to come by bike? Had he fallen down in a gutter somewhere, or was he already staggering at the head of some posse of townies heading for the island with burning torches to apprehend the Dog Killer?

No matter. I would see anybody coming, even in this light, and could go out to welcome my brother or escape the house to hide out on the island if the vigilantes appeared. I turned the radio off so I could hear any shouts from the mainland, and strained my eyes to search through the fading light. After a while I raced down to the kitchen and got a small packed meal together and stuffed it into a canvas bag in the loft. It was just in case I did have to leave the house and did meet Eric. He might be hungry. I settled into the seat, scanning the shadows over the darkening land. In the far distance, at the base of the hills, lights moved on the road, glittering in the dusk, flashing like irregular lighthouses through the trees, round corners, over hills. I rubbed my eyes and stretched, trying to get the weariness out of my system.

I thought ahead, added some painkillers to the bag I would take out of the house if I had to. This sort of weather might bring on Eric's migraine, and he might need some relief. I hoped he didn't have one.

I yawned, widened my eyes, ate another apple. The vague shadows under the clouds turned darker.

I woke up.

It was dark, I was still in the chair, arms crossed under my head, resting on the metal surround of the skylight. And something, a noise inside the house, had woken me. I sat for a second, feeling my heart race, feeling my back complain about the position it had been in for so long. Blood made its painful way into the parts of my arms the weight of my head had restricted the supply to. I spun round in the chair, quickly and quietly. The loft was black, but I didn't sense anything. I touched a button on my watch, discovered it was after eleven. I had slept for hours. Idiot! Then I heard somebody moving about downstairs; indistinct footsteps, a door closing, other noises. Glass smashed. I felt the hair on the back of my neck go up; the second time in one week. I clenched my jaw, told myself to stop taking fright and *do something.* It might be Eric or it might be my father. I would go down and find out. To be safe, I would take my knife.

I got off the seat, went carefully to where the door was, feeling my way round the roughness of the chimney bricks. I stopped there, took the tail of my shirt out and let it hang over my cords, concealing the knife where it hung from my belt. I eased myself silently down into the dark landing. A light was on in the hall, right at the bottom, and it cast strange sets of shadows, yellow and dim, up over the landing walls. I went along to the banisters, looked over the rail. I couldn't see anything. The noises had stopped. I sniffed the air.

I could smell the smoky, pubby smell of drink. It must be my father. I felt relieved. Just then I heard him come out of the lounge. A noise washed out behind him like an ocean roaring. I came away from the rail and stood listening. He was staggering, bumping off the walls and tripping on the stairs. I heard him breathing heavily and muttering something. I listened, let the smell and sound come up. I stood and gradually I calmed myself. I heard my father get to the first

169

landing, where the phone was. Then unsteady footsteps.

'Frang!' he shouted. I kept still, said nothing. Just instinct, I suppose, or habit born of all the times I've pretended not to be where I really am, and listened to people when they have thought they were alone. I breathed slowly.

'*Frang!*' he yelled. I got ready to go back up to the loft, shifting back, on tip-toe, avoiding the places where I knew the floor creaked. My father hammered on the door of the first-floor toilet, then cursed when he discovered it was open. I heard him start up the stairs, towards me. His steps pattered, irregular, and he grunted as he stumbled and hit a wall. I went quietly up the ladder, swung up and on to the bare wood floor of the loft, lay there with my head a metre or so from the hole, my hands on the brickwork, ready to duck behind the flue if my father attempted to look into the loft from the hole. I blinked. My father hammered on my room door. He opened it.

'Frang! he shouted again. Then 'Ah . . . fuck. . . .'

My heart leaped as I lay there. I had never heard him swear before. It sounded obscene in his mouth, not like the casual way Eric or Jamie said it. I heard him breathing under the hole, the smell of him coming up through it to me: whisky and tobacco.

The steps again, unsteady down the landing, then his door, and it slamming shut. I breathed again, only then realising that I had been holding my breath. My heart was pounding fit to burst and I was almost surprised my father hadn't been able to hear it booming through the floorboards above him. I waited for a while, but there were no more noises, just that distant white sound from the lounge. It sounded as though he had left the television on, between channels.

I lay there, gave him five minutes, then I got up slowly, brushed myself down, tucked my shirt in, picked up the bag in the darkness, attached my catapult to my belt, felt around for my waistcoat and found it, then with all my gear on crept down the ladder and on to the landing, then along it and softly downstairs.

In the lounge, the television sparkled its colourful hiss to an empty room. I went to it, clicked it off. I turned to go and saw my father's tweed jacket lying crumpled in a chair. I picked it up and it jingled. I felt through the pockets as I wrinkled my nose at the stench of drink and smoke coming off it. My hand closed around a bunch of keys.

I brought them out and stared at them. There was the front-door key, the back-door key, the cellar key, shed key, a couple of smaller ones I didn't recognise, and another key, a key to one of the rooms in the house, like the key for my room but a different cut. I felt my mouth start to dry up, and saw my hand start to shake in front of me. Sweat sparkled on it, beading suddenly in the lines of the palm. It might be his bedroom key or. . . .

I ran upstairs, three at a time, only breaking rhythm for the noisy ones. I went up past the study, up to my father's bedroom. The door was ajar, its key was in the lock. I could hear my father snoring. I closed the door gently and ran back down to the study. I put the key in the lock, and it turned with well-oiled ease. I stood there for a second or two, then turned the handle, opened the door.

I put the light on. The study.

It was cluttered and full, stuffy and warm. The light in the centre of the ceiling had no shade, and was very bright. There were two desks, a bureau, and a camp bed with a mess of sheets lying twisted on it. There was a bookcase, two large tables standing together covered with various bottles and pieces of chemical apparatus; test tubes and bottles and a condenser linked to a sink in the corner. The place smelled of something like ammonia. I turned, stuck my head out of the door into the hall, listened, heard very distant snoring, then took the key and closed the door, locking myself in and leaving the key in the door.

It was as I turned away from the door that I saw it. A specimen-jar standing on top of the bureau, which was placed just to the side of the door and would be hidden from the hall outside by the door when it was open. In the jar was clear liquid – alcohol, I assumed. In the alcohol was a tiny, torn set of male genitalia.

I looked at it, my hand still on the key I had been turning, and my eyes filled. I felt something in my throat, something from deep in me, and my eyes and nose seemed to fill and quickly burst. I stood and I cried, letting the tears trickle down my cheeks and into my mouth, salting it. My nose ran, and I sniffed and snorted, and I felt my chest heave and a muscle in my jaw tremored uncontrollably. I forgot all about Eric, about my father, about everything except me, and my loss.

It took me some time to pull myself together, and I didn't do it by being angry at myself or telling myself not to act like some stupid girl, but I just calmed down naturally and evenly, and some sort of weight left my head and settled in my stomach. I wiped my face on my shirt and blew my nose quietly, then started searching the room methodically, ignoring the jar on the bureau. Maybe that was all the secret there was, but I wanted to be sure.

Most of it was junk. Junk and chemicals. The drawers of the desk and the bureau were filled with ancient photographs and papers. There were old letters, old bills and notes, deeds and forms and insurance policies (none for me, and all expired long since anyway), pages from a short story or novel somebody had been writing on a cheap typewriter, covered in corrections and still awful (something about hippies in a commune in the desert somewhere making contact with aliens); there were glass paperweights, gloves, psychedelic badges, some old Beatles singles, a few copies of *Oz* and *IT*, some dry pens and broken pencils. Rubbish, all rubbish.

Then I came to part of the bureau which was locked: one section under the roll-top hinged at the bottom with a keyhole in the top edge. I got the keys from the door and, sure enough, one of the small ones fitted. The flap hinged down and I took out the four small drawers set behind it and set them on the working-surface of the bureau.

I stared at their contents until my legs got shaky and I had to sit down on the rickety little chair which had been half-underneath the bureau. I put my head in my hands and I was shaking again. How much was I going to have to go through this night?

172

I put my hands into one of the little drawers and took out the blue box of tampons. Shaking fingers brought out the other box from the drawer. It was labelled 'Hormones – male'. Inside it were smaller boxes, neatly numbered in black biro with dates going about six months into the future. Another box from a different drawer said 'KBr', which rang a bell somewhere in my mind, but only at the very back of it. The remaining two drawers contained tightly rolled bundles of five- and ten-pound notes and Cellophane bags with little squares of paper inside. I had no spare capacity for trying to work out what any of that other stuff was, though; my mind was racing with an awful idea it had just formed. I sat there, staring, mouth open, and I thought. I didn't look up at the jar.

I thought of that delicate face, those lightly haired arms. I tried to think of one time I had seen my father naked to the waist, but for the life of me I couldn't. The secret. It couldn't be. I shook my head, but I couldn't let go of the idea. Angus. Agnes. I only had his word for anything that had happened. I had no idea at all how much Mrs Clamp could be trusted, no idea what sort of hold either of them might have over the other. But it *couldn't* be! It was just so monstrous, so appalling! I stood up quickly, letting the chair fall back and whack on the wood of the uncovered boards. I grabbed the box of tampons and the hormones, took the keys, unlocked the door and charged out, upstairs, stuffing the keys into one pocket and drawing my knife from its sheath. 'Frank'll get you,' I hissed to myself.

I stormed into my father's room and swtiched on the light. He was lying on the bed with his clothes on. One shoe was off; it lay on the floor under his foot, which dangled over the side of the bed. He was on his back, snoring. He stirred and flung one arm over his face, turning away from the light. I went over to him, took the arm away and slapped his face twice, hard. His head shook, and he cried out. One eye, then the other, opened. I put the knife up to his eyes, watching them focus on it with drunken imprecision. The smell of drink off him was foul.

'Frang?' he said weakly. I jabbed the knife at him, just

stopping short of the bridge of his nose.

'You bastard,' I spat at him. 'What the hell are these?' I brandished the tampons and the hormones box in front of him with my other hand. He groaned and closed his eyes. 'Tell me!' I screamed, and slapped him again, using the back of the hand holding the knife. He tried to roll away from me, across the bed under the open window, but I pulled him back from the hot, still night.

'No, Frang, no,' he said, shaking his head and trying to push my hands away. I let the boxes go and got hold of him by one arm, tightly. I drew him near to me, pointed the knife at his throat.

'You're going to tell me, or by God. . . .' I let the words hang. I let go of his arm and moved my hand down to his trousers. I slipped his belt out of the little guides round the waist. He tried to stop me in a fumbling way, but I slapped his hands back and prodded him in the throat with the knife. I undid the belt and pulled the zip down, watching him all the time, trying not to imagine what I might find, what I might *not* find. I undid the button at the top of the zip. I pulled his trousers open, pulled his shirt up and out. He looked at me, lying on the bed with his eyes red and gleaming, and he shook his head.

'Wha' you goin' t'do, Frangie? Am sorry, am really really sorry. Was an experimen, sall. Juss an experimen. . . . Don' do anything' t'me, please, Frangie. . . . Please. . . .'

'You bitch, you *bitch*!' I said, feeling my eyes start to blur and my voice shake. I pulled his/her underpants down with a vicious tug.

Something screamed outside, in the night beyond the window. I stood staring at my father's dark-haired, large, rather greasy-looking cock and balls, and something animal, out there on the landscape of the island, screamed. My father's legs were quivering. Then came a light, orange and wavering, where no light should be, out there, over the dunes, and more screams, bleatings and baas and screams; everywhere screams.

'Jesus Christ, what's that?' my father breathed, turning a shaking head towards the window. I stood back, then went

174

past the bottom of the bed, looking out of the window. The awful noises and the light on the far side of the dunes seemed to be coming closer. The light was in a halo over the big dune behind the house, where the Skull Grounds were; it was flickering yellow with smoke-trails in it. The noise was like that the burning dog had made, but magnified, repeated and repeated, and with another edge to it. The light grew stronger, and something came running over the top of the big dune, something burning and screaming and running down over the sea-face of the Skull Grounds dune. It was a sheep, and it was followed by more. First another two, then half a dozen animals came charging over the grass and the sand. In seconds the hillside was covered with burning sheep, their wool in flames, bleating wildly and running down the hill, lighting up the sandy grass and weeds and leaving them burning in their fiery wake.

And then I saw Eric. My father came shakily up by my side, but I ignored him and watched the skinny, dancing, leaping figure on the very top of the dune. Eric was waving a huge burning torch in one hand and an axe in the other. He was screaming, too.

'Oh, my God, no,' my father said. I turned to him. He was pulling his trousers up. I pushed past him and ran to the door.

'Come on,' I shouted at him. I went out, ran downstairs, not waiting to see if he was following. I could see flames through every window, hear the wails of the tortured sheep all around the house. I got to the kitchen, considered getting some water as I ran through, but decided it was pointless. I ran out through the porch and into the garden. A sheep, burning only above its back legs, nearly collided with me, running through the already blazing garden and swerving at the last second from the door with a terrified baaing, then jumping over the low fence into the front garden. I ran round the back of the house, looking for Eric.

Sheep were everywhere, fire was all about. The grass over the Skull Grounds was ablaze, flames leaped from the shed and the bushes and the plants and flowers in the garden, and dead, burning sheep lay in pools of livid fire while others ran and jumped about, moaning and howling in their guttural,

175

broken voices. Eric was down the steps leading to the cellar. I saw the torch he had been holding, flickering flame against the wall of the house beneath the window to the downstairs toilet. He was attacking the door to the cellar with the axe.

'Eric! No!' I screamed. I started forward, then turned, grabbed the edge of the house and stuck my head round the corner to look at the open door of the porch. 'Dad! Get out of the house! Dad!' I could hear the sound of splintering wood behind me. I turned and ran for Eric. I jumped over the smouldering carcass of a sheep just before the cellar steps. Eric turned round and swung the axe at me. I ducked and rolled. I landed and jumped up, ready to spring away, but he was back smashing the axe into the door again, screaming with each massive blow as though he was the door. The axe head disappeared through the wood, became stuck; he wriggled it mightily and got it out, glanced back at me and then heaved the axe at the door again. The flames from the torch threw his shadow at me; the torch lay propped against the side of the door and I could see the new paint had started burning already. I got my catapult out. Eric had the door almost down. My father still hadn't shown. Eric glanced back at me again then smashed the axe into the door. A sheep cried out behind us as I fumbled for a steelie. I could hear the crackling of fires on all sides and smell roasted meat. The metal sphere fitted into the leather and I pulled.

'Eric!' I yelled, as the door gave way. He held the axe with one hand, picked up the torch with the other; he kicked the door and it fell. I tensed the catapult one final centimetre. I gazed at him through the Y of the catapult's arms. He looked at me. His face was bearded, dirty, like an animal mask. It was the boy, the man I had known, and it was another person entirely. That face was grinning and leering and sweating, and it beat to and fro as his chest heaved in and out and the flames pulsed. He held the axe and the burning brand, and the cellar door lay in a wreck behind him. I thought I could just make out the bales of cordite, darkly orange in the thick and shivering light from the fires around us and the torch my brother held. He shook his head, looking expectant and confused.

176

I shook my head, slowly.

He laughed and nodded, half-dropped, half-threw the torch into the cellar, and ran at me.

I almost released the steelie as I saw him come at me through the catapult, but just in the last second before my fingers opened I saw he had dropped the axe; it clattered off the steps to the cellar as Eric dodged past me and I dropped and ducked to one side. I rolled, saw Eric haring away over the garden, heading south down the island. I dropped the catapult, ran down the steps and picked the torch up. It was a metre into the cellar, nowhere near the bales. I threw it outside quickly as the bombs in the blazing shed started to go off.

The noise was deafening, shrapnel whizzed over my head, windows in the house blew in and the shed was totally demolished; a couple of bombs were blown out of the shed and exploded in other parts of the garden, but luckily none came near me. By the time it was safe for me to raise my head the shed no longer existed, all the sheep were dead or gone, and Eric had vanished.

My father was in the kitchen, holding a pail of water and a carving-knife. I came in and he put the knife down on the table. He looked about a hundred years old. On the table was the specimen-jar. I sat down at the head of the table, collapsing into the chair. I looked at him.

'That was Eric at the door, Dad,' I said, and laughed. My ears were still ringing from the explosions in the shed.

My father stood looking old and stupid, and his eyes were bleary and wet and his hands shook. I felt myself calm down, gradually.

'Wha—' he began, then cleared his throat. 'What . . . what happened?' He sounded almost sober.

'He tried to get into the cellar. I think he was going to blow us all up. He's run off now. I've put the door back up as best I can. Most of the fires are out; you won't need that.' I nodded at the pail of water he held. 'Instead I'd like you to sit down and tell me one or two things I'd like to know.' I sat back in my chair.

He looked at me for a second, then he picked up the specimen-jar, but it slipped from his fingers, fell to the floor and smashed. He gave a nervous laugh, bent, and stood back up holding what had been inside the jar. He held it out for me to see, but I was looking into his face. He closed his hand, then opened it again, like a magician. He was holding a pink ball. Not a testicle; a pink ball, like a lump of plasticine, or wax. I stared back into his eyes.

'Tell me,' I said.

So he told me.

12: What Happened to Me

ONCE, far south, past even the new house, I went to build some dams amongst the sand and the rock pools on that part of the coast. It was a perfect, calm, luminous day. There was no line between the sea and the sky, and any smoke rose straight. The sea was flat.

On the land in the distance there were some fields, set on to a mildly sloping hillside. In one field there were some cows and two big brown horses. While I was building, a lorry came down a track by the field. It stopped by the gate, reversed and turned so that its rear was facing me. I watched through the binoculars as this went on about half a mile away. Two men got out. They opened the back of the truck so that a ramp was formed into its interior, wooden slatted sides being folded out to make fences on either side of the ramp. The two horses came to watch.

I stood in a rock pool, water round my wellingtons, and I cast a watery shadow. The men went into the field and led one of the horses out, a rope round its neck. It went out with no complaint, but when the men tried to get it to go into the truck, up the tailboard, between the skewed, slatted sides, it shied and refused, leaned backwards. Its mate pressed against the fence beside it. I heard its cries, seconds late through the still air. The horse would not go in. Some cows in the field looked on, then continued munching.

Tiny waves, clear folds of light, consumed the sand, rock, weed and shell beside me, lapping quietly. A bird called in the calmness. The men moved the truck away, led the horse after it, down the track and along an offshoot of it. The horse in the field cried out, and ran in pointless circles. My arms and eyes grew tired, and I looked away, at the line of hills and mountains marching into the glowing light of the north. When I looked back they had the horse inside the truck.

The truck moved off, wheels spinning briefly. The lone horse, confused again, ran from gate to fence and back again, first following the truck, then not. One of the men had stayed behind in the field with it, and as the truck disappeared over the brow of the hill he calmed the animal.

Later, on my way back home, I passed the field with the horse in it, and it was quietly cropping the grass.

I am sitting on the dune above the Bunker now, in this fresh, breezy Sunday morning, and I am remembering dreaming about that horse last night.

After my father told me what he had to tell me, and I passed through disbelief and fury to stunned acceptance, and after we had a look round the outskirts of the garden, calling for Eric, cleaning up the mess the best we could and putting out the remaining small fires, after we barricaded the cellar door and went back to the house and he told me why he had done what he had, we went to bed. I locked my bedroom door, and I'm pretty sure he locked his. I slept, had a dream in which I relived that evening of the horses, then woke early and went out, looking for Eric. I saw Diggs coming down the path as I left. My father had a lot of talking to do. I left them to it.

The weather had cleared. No storm, no thunder and lightning, just a wind out of the west sweeping all the cloud away out to sea, and the worst of the heat with it. Like a miracle, though more likely just an anticyclone over Norway. So it was bright and clear and cool.

I found Eric lying asleep on the dune above the Bunker, head in the swaying grass, curled up like a little child. I went up to him and sat beside him for a while, then spoke his name, nudged his shoulder. He woke up, looked at me and smiled.

'Hello, Eric,' I said. He held out one hand and I clasped it. He nodded, still smiling. Then he shifted, put his curly head on my lap, closed his eyes and went to sleep.

I'm not Francis Leslie Cauldhame. I'm Frances Lesley Cauldhame. That's what it boils down to. The tampons and the hormones were for me.

My father dressing Eric up as a girl was just, as it turned out, a rehearsal for me. When Old Saul savaged me, my father saw it as an ideal opportunity for a little experiment, and a way of lessening – perhaps removing entirely – the influence of the female around him as I grew up. So he started dosing me with male hormones, and has been ever since. That's why he's always made the meals, that's why what I've always thought was the stump of a penis is really an enlarged clitoris. Hence the beard, no periods, and all the rest.

But he has kept tampons for the last few years, just in case my own hormones got the better of the ones he had been pumping me with. He had the bromide to stop the added androgen making me feel randy. He made a fake set of male genitals from the same wax kit I found under the stairs and made my candles from. He was going to confront me with the specimen-jar if I ever started to query whether I really was castrated. More proof; more lies. Even the stuff about farting was a cheat; he's been friends with Duncan the barman for years and buys him drinks in return for an informative phone call after I've been drinking in the Arms. Even now I can't be sure he's told me everything, though he did seem to be gripped by the urge to confess all, and tears were in his eyes last night.

Thinking about it, I feel a knot of anger building in my stomach again, but I fight it. I wanted to kill him, there and then in the kitchen after he told me and convinced me. Part of me still wants to believe it's just his latest lie, but really I know it's the truth. I'm a woman. Scarred thighs, outer labia a bit chewed up, and I'll never be attractive, but according to Dad a normal female, capable of intercourse and giving birth (I shiver at the thought of either).

I look out at the glittering sea while Eric's head rests on my lap and I think again of that poor horse.

I don't know what I'm going to do. I can't stay here, and I'm frightened of everywhere else. But I suppose I'll have to go. What a bummer. Maybe I'd consider suicide, if some of my relatives hadn't produced such difficult acts to follow.

I look down at Eric's head: quiet, dirty, asleep. His face is calm. He feels no pain.

I watched the small waves fall on the beach for a while. On the sea, on that lens of water, twice-bulged and wobbling and rolling around the earth, I am looking at a rippled desert, and I have seen it as flat as a salt lake. Elsewhere the geography is different; the sea undulates, sways and swells, folds into rolling downs under freshening breezes, piles into foothills beneath the stiffening trades, and finally rears white-topped and blizzard-streaked in circling mountain ranges rammed by the storm-forced wind.

And where I am, where we sit and lie and sleep and look, on this warm summer's day, the snow will fall in a half-year's time. The ice and frost, the rime and hoar, the howling gale born in Siberia, pushed over Scandinavia and swept across the North Sea, the world's grey waters and the air's dun skies will lay their cold, determined hands on this place, make it theirs for a while.

I want to laugh or cry or both, as I sit here, thinking about my one life, my three deaths. Four deaths now, in a way, now that my father's truth has murdered what I was.

But I *am* still me; I *am* the same person, with the same memories and the same deeds done, the same (small) achievements, the same (appalling) crimes to *my* name.

Why? *How* could I have done those things?

Perhaps it was because I thought I had had all that really mattered in the world, the whole reason – and means – for our continuance as a species, stolen from me before I even knew its value. Perhaps I murdered for revenge in each case, jealously exacting – through the only potency at my command – a toll from those who passed within my range; my peers who each would otherwise have grown into the one thing I could never become: an adult.

Lacking, as one might say, one will, I forged another; to lick my own wound, I cut *them* off, reciprocating in my angry innocence the emasculation I could not then fully appreciate, but somehow – through the attitudes of others perhaps – sensed as an unfair, irrecoverable loss. Having no purpose in life or procreation, I invested all my worth in that grim opposite, and so found a negative and negation of the fecundity only others could lay claim to. I believe that I decided if I could never become a man, I – the unmanned – would out-man those around me, and so I became the killer, a small image of the ruthless soldier-hero almost all I've ever seen or read seems to pay strict homage to. I would find or make my own weapons, and my victims would be those most recently produced by the one act I was incapable of; my equals in that, while they possessed the potential for generation, they were at that point no more able to perform the required act than I was. Talk about penis envy.

Now it all turns out to have been for nothing. There was no revenge that needed taking, only a lie, a trick that should have been exposed, a disguise which even from the inside I should have seen through, but in the end did not want to. I was proud; eunuch but unique; a fierce and noble presence in my lands, a crippled warrior, fallen prince. . . .

Now I find I was the fool all along.

Believing in my great hurt, my literal cutting off from society's mainland, it seems to me that I took life in a sense too seriously, and the lives of others, for the same reason, too lightly. The murders were my own conception; my sex. The Factory was my attempt to construct life, to replace the involvement which otherwise I did not want.

Well, it is always easier to succeed at death.

Inside this greater machine, things are not quite so cut and dried (or cut and pickled) as they have appeared in my experience. Each of us, in our own personal Factory, may

183

believe we have stumbled down one corridor, and that our fate is sealed and certain (dream or nightmare, humdrum or bizarre, good or bad), but a word, a glance, a slip – anything can change that, alter it entirely, and our marble hall becomes a gutter, or our rat-maze a golden path. Our destination is the same in the end, but our journey – part chosen, part determined – is different for us all, and changes even as we live and grow. I thought one door had snicked shut behind me years ago; in fact I was still crawling about the face. *Now* the door closes, and my journey begins.

I look down at Eric again, and smile, nod to myself in the breeze while the waves break and the wind moves spray and grass and a few birds call. I suppose I'll have to tell him what's happened to me.

Poor Eric came home to see his brother, only to find (Zap! Pow! Dams burst! Bombs go off! Wasps fry: *ttssss*!) he's got a sister.